Y0-BZG-819

". . . It's not a single corporation we're after. It's the system. It's the system that killed our men and our way of life. It's the system that's got to go."

She went on, and her voice had a dreamy quality to it. "It's not even just that the system has to go. It's the system we're going to kill. Us. With our bare hands if we could. With our bare asses since we can't. We're murderers and we're pragmatists. But the murderer part comes first. With each and every one of us. Killers. Deadly. And deadly with purpose."

"Dublin," she said quietly, "you're just a revolutionist. But revolution is addictive. One whets your appetite. Two will addict you more. . . ."

GALLAGHER'S GLACIER

...of Walt (1922—1977)

..."That deep, ringing voice that I heard—that *cheee-ops, cheee-ops, cheee-ops* of an upside-down Solar Tap—was a freedom bell ringing across the starways—modern, ruthless, *impertinent* to stupidity ... and I knew that it's men that make history, not history that makes a man. For it takes a man not only to dream freedom for mankind, but to make it possible...."

...and Leigh

Aboard the C-Lab
Rathmann's Marina
705 S. Harbor City Blvd.
Melbourne, Florida 32901

May, 1979

GALLAGHER'S GLACIER

WALT and LEIGH RICHMOND

THE ORIGINAL, UNCUT VERSION

SF
ace books

A Division of Charter Communications Inc.
A GROSSET & DUNLAP COMPANY
360 Park Avenue South
New York, New York 10010

Copyright © 1970 by Walt and Leigh Richmond
All material new to this edition copyright © 1979
by The Centric Foundation, Inc.

All rights reserved. No part of this book may be reproduced in any form or by any means, except for the inclusion of brief quotations in a review, without permission in writing from the publisher.

All characters in this book are fictitious. Any resemblance to actual persons, living or dead, is purely coincidental.

An ACE Book

Cover art by John Rush

This Ace printing: July 1979

Printed in U.S.A.

ONE

The thing about history is, it's hard to tell whether men make history or history makes men.

Take Gallagher and his glacier. Now, you might say that he changed history; and then again, you may figure that history would have changed anyhow, that he just happened to be the guy in the spot at the time. I wouldn't know. He was a colorful character, and that's what did the changing in some ways. History needs its Paul Bunyans.

You see, when men first went out into space, the mortality was terrific, but the corporations survived. Men die, and when they're independents, that's that; but when they're representatives of a corporation, the corporation can follow them up with more men and more, and the corporation stays alive.

People get to thinking that only corporations belong in space, and they act accordingly. And pretty soon space is all tied up in pretty blue corporate ribbons, and it's not really a pioneering venture. A man doesn't stand so tall, out there in the stars. And the colonies learn to obey the corporate rules.

That was the way it was going, and going fast. But the corporations had one drawback: they leaned toward the bright young technicians like me, with lots of degrees and very little know-how.

In space what you really need—it took me a long time to find this out—is what some people call horse sense. You need the ability to translate what's in a book into what makes sense when it's right before you. You need to do your own looking. You use all that book-learning as a sort of tool, but only as a tool. You need to meet a problem head-on—for what it is, not what the book says it's supposed to be.

That kind of man, though, isn't the kind the coporations can hire, even when they want to—which they normally don't. That kind of man is an independent, and in the battle for the profits that makes it possible for a man to stay in space, the bright young corporate men are likelier to win.

That's where you find the frictions. For the independents may die in droves, as they did conquering space, but there'll be some that live; and those that stay alive are a hardier lot. Even in the company colonies, the ones that stayed alive from the beginning—the ones that didn't have to be replaced—had a look about them and a way about them, and even the company talked softly to them when it made its rules.

So maybe it wasn't Gallagher at all. Maybe it was the times and how a man develops in space, and he was just the man who happened to fit the circumstances.

Now, you might think that space is so big that you could have the bright young men of the corporations and their seemingly endless replacements; and you could have the independent types that managed to survive after all, and no bother about friction between them. But you'd be wrong. Space is big, but the meeting places are common to both, and the frictions are very real.

It got to be pretty much of a standoff. The independents who survived had that one common ingredient—horse sense, you could call it; or know-how—and it was a needed thing on the planets. And the corporations could send in all the bright young men they liked to control their colonies; it was the surviving independents with the horse sense who did the controlling where the colonies paid off.

But the corporations controlled the ships, and they were push-button ships those days. You didn't need horse sense. So the bright young technicians—yes, I was one of them—who knew it all and didn't need to be taught anything by space itself, controlled the ships. And it was a trading economy.

It took a pile of cash to buy a ship and a pile of equipment to build one, and as far as anyone could see, it would be a long, cold year in hell before the independents could master their own fleets and break the hold of the corporations.

So it would be a long, cold year in hell before the frictions left. Meanwhile, you'd better go into port at least three strong men together and stay together. That's how it was, and you'd think that was how it was going to be from now on.

So maybe it *was* Gallagher and his glacier that changed the times, and not the times that fitted Gallagher.

A pioneer is a man who goes out into the unknown and solves equations to the best of his ability as he meets them. In that respect, Gallagher was a pioneer, and I knew that in that respect I wasn't. That hurt the ever-living soul of me, underneath all the degrees and certificates that said I was captain of a ship and he wasn't.

An engineer is a man who gets a job done, and in that respect Gallagher was an engineer. I didn't know whether I was an engineer or not, for I had the book learning, but the ship was a push-button affair that took some handling but that mostly took automatics; and the Port Inspector was the one who said how the automatics would be structured. Gallagher had as good a piece of paper to prove he was an engineer as I did, but he held that piece of paper in great contempt, except when he needed a job, which was a good part of the time since, though he was an engineer with a spacelanes-long reputation, he never had developed a talent for staying on a company ship. As a pioneer, he never had been able to latch onto a colony, company, or otherwise, and stay, for he had a sociable nature that needed to be out and visiting around the spaceways.

Gallagher's name was black in the company books. He'd jump a ship or stow away out of a colony as soon as sign the papers.

So now he sat, mostly in Joe's Bar, and waited for a ship to orbit that was setting a course the way he wanted to go. How he was planning to sign on with his name so black in the books, he wasn't saying.

But when my ship orbited, and us heading for Altura, there was a small series of untraceable incidents that left my engineer in the hospital. At the same time, I got the news of the "incidents," Gallagher presented himself shipside with his piece of paper.

"Your next port is Altura, Captain Harald Dundee," he said proud-like. His name was N. N. Gallagher, and they called him "Dublin" as a pun and for courtesy of his origin. He stood six feet tall in my cabin, his red hair nearly brushing the topsides, making me feel small and a little insignificant for all my fine uniform, for I clear that ceiling by a good four inches.

"And," he said, "it's toward Altura I'm headin'. Now, seeing as it's not rightly your fault you're minus an engineer for the course, I'll take on the job without much cost to you. There's a glacier that's orbiting towards Altura. You can compute to intersect her within three hours of your port. I'll take on your engineer's post that far and charge you naught, if you'll put me aboard that glacier, me and my equipment. And your assistant engineer can take her in from there."

Well, I was a young man then, and my first command—all spit and polish and by-the-book. I didn't like that proposition. I didn't even right-ly believe it, though there wasn't anything about it to disbelieve. I had heard that, though Gallagher might be footloose and black in the books, he could engineer a ship like the angel of machines sent straight for the purpose.

I turned him down with a cold rejection that would have been an insult if he'd been looking for insults which were easy enough to find in any port—as I said, the frictions being what they were. It wasn't the sort of thing you did, I told him curtly, horsetrading engineering for passage.

So he turned on his heel and he left with a half-smile. Within two hours, I knew what that half-smile meant. There wouldn't be another engineer available in that port, I found out soon enough, and I could knuckle under to his proposition—which I knew to be blackmail—or I could argue the point and wait out the next ship through to bring me an engineer and forget the tight, company-set schedule on which I was operating.

I swallowed my pride and started to send along a messenger to fetch the man back. Then I thought twice, put on my best uniform, and made my way into the port town. If he refused the messenger, I would have to go to him or run late with the company, and company records being what they are, knew I'd better not run late—me, a young man with my first commission.

In my best uniform, and unaccompanied, though the custom was for not less than three to go ashore together in any port in space, I headed for Joe's Bar. I could spy his red hair from the entranceway, but I pretended not to see him and sat down three stools away.

I drank the first two drinks slow and easy and watched from the corner of my eye that Gallagher paced me drink for drink. Then I spoke aloud to the bartender, and I called him Joe through courtesy to the title of his bar, though his accent was guttural and it didn't seem likely that the name Joe had ever been used in any christening of his.

"Joe," says I, stumbling over the words just a bit to show I'd been consuming, "my ship's out there with the sweetest motors that all the technical brains of Earth could put into her. These guys they call engineers are just racketeers," I said loud-like. "There's not a thing they can do to a motor to make it purr more sweetly than the designer intended. They just figure to go along for the ride, for it don't take a man to push the buttons."

By the time I'd finished, that red hair was standing on end, and there was no pretense about whether Gallagher was listening. But he gulped a couple of times and bit his tongue. When he finally spoke, it was in the brogue and soft-like, and he had his temper where he wanted it; pushing from beneath but not pulling out ahead.

"Mister," says Gallagher, "or perhaps I should say 'captain'—though button pushers never seemed to me to rate that title—you show me the drive that I can't tune, and I'll pay you for the privilege of shipping me as engineer for three times five ports, and not jump your ship.

There's not a drive operating in a company ship since the corporations took over the shipping lanes that couldn't stand the touch of Gallagher," says he, "and fly so much sweeter because of that touch that even her imbecile master would be forced to admit it, though it cost him his pride—if he had honor to boot."

Now no man impugns my honor, and I was on my feet looking up into that grinning Irish mug of his, my fists doubled.

"Set down, captain," says he quietly. "Let's talk this over polite-like, for it was a good ploy and it's got me abroad the *Starfire*—me *and* my equipment."

Well, that was that, but when I found out what Gallagher meant by *equipment,* I nearly reneged again. The holds would take it, but we'd be shipping heavy.

"You'll be heavy only so long as I'm aboard, and I'll have your drive talking so pretty she'll use less mass than if you were running light with anybody else to engineer her," says Gallagher modestly. "Your assistant will have a light ship to take in, and the motors already purring."

The equipment included one of the old Antolaric drives that used to power the ships they sent out when man first entered space, and it was as massive as the old ships used to be. Then there were supplies to last a man for months, but those weren't much; and machinery enough to stock a small shop.

Well, I was stuck with it, but that didn't make me like it. I liked it even less when he demanded —he didn't ask, he demanded, but I ignored the manner of his request—twenty-four hours to work on the drive before we lifted.

When we lifted, I didn't begrudge a minute of that twenty-four hours. The *Starfire* acted like a thing alive, tuned to my every motion. I changed from worrying over what he'd been doing during that twenty-four hours to worrying whether the changes in the engineering setup could be justified to a port inspection engineer, even though the results were such as captains dream of. Port inspection engineers are the brightest of the bright young men, and I knew my breed and its shortcomings. That drive wasn't tuned by the book. It wouldn't pass.

I didn't understand Gallagher, but I knew him for a breed that caught at the heart of me, for we were both from the old country and we were both out in the new spaceways. There was a kinship between us I couldn't deny, though the frictions said we were alien, and me a corporation man.

I understood the man even less when we matched courses with his glacier and I had him and his equipment drifted over to it. It couldn't have been more than a mile the long way, and a quarter mile through; an ungainly hunk of ice idling through space. What the man could want with it was more than I could see. There were plenty of steel meteorites that size, if Gallagher wanted to make himself a meteor ship—and I admit that seeing that old drive was the first inkling I'd got of such a use. But ice? Then I realized. A steel meteor wouldn't have given him reaction mass for his fusion chamber, but that ice was a good part hydrogen, and that would be his mass.

We blasted on for Altura, and I spent my best wiles—and the finest whisky I could buy—on the port inspection engineer, but to little avail. That ship had to be retuned before we blasted again, and he wouldn't even test-blast with me so I could let him handle a ship when it was tuned the way the *Starfire* was tuned now. It wasn't by the book, and be damned to me. He had a few cutting things to say about what would be in my records that I'd let a man like Gallagher manhandle my drive.

Well, I'd be a few days planetbound, and I spent the first of them partly wandering the company town, partly in the port bar. By the end of the fourth day, I was so furious with Gallagher that I was making up conversations with him, telling him off. And, if you come right down to it, curious. I couldn't figure how he was going to manage the job alone. I had to see.

By midnight I'd rationalized myself into good reasons. The man was daft. He was alone on an iceberg, drifting helplessly in space. By now he'd have realized how helplessly. The least I could do—now that his senses had had a chance to re-organize—was to offer him an oiler's job to get him out of the mess he'd talked himself into. I wouldn't leave a dog alone out there, I told myself. I owed him a chance to stow away honorably.

I rented a small interplanet scout, and I headed back for Gallagher's glacier.

What I expected to find I'm not sure. What I

found was the glacier—lonely and sparkling cold —and I could make out Gallagher's vac-suited figure working on its surface as I matched orbit two kilometers off.

Since he was on the surface and in a vac suit, I hailed him over the ship's suit comm, but he failed to answer, and I maneuvered the scout in closer, seeking a place to tie up. That's when I got an answer.

"Sheer off, you lunkhead," came his voice. "I'll not have you upsetting my balances here."

I was readying a tart reply when he went on. "Anyhow, this is already claimed."

"Okay, Dublin," I said. "If you're too proud to let your former captain see the mess you've got into, I'll be heading back to port. I was just being sociable anyhow."

The figure stood and waved, and Gallagher's tones, hardly less gruff than before, came back over the suit comm. "Neighborly of you, captain. Take her around on the far side and hitch up to a mooring line. But gently, mind you. I'll still not have you upsetting my balance."

I was blessed if I could see what he might have in mind about balances, but I eased the scout around to the far side, and that's when I got my first good look at what Gallagher had been doing.

There was a bubble dome anchored firmly to one of the smoother parts of the big ice chunk, and a half-dozen standard bourdon mooring tubes—long, snaky pipes of plastic inflated with gas—that extended out from the surface and to which various "dumps" had been attached. The bubble dome was fair enough; normal equipment for airless planetary living. And the bourdon mooring tubes were normal, *if* they were attached securely enough to the iceberg.

I hesitated before mooring to a vacant tube. They'd attach to the scout all right; and if they were moored securely at the far end, fine. But if they weren't? Well, I'd moor, I decided, and keep an eye on the scout. If it pulled the line loose and started to drift, I could catch it in the first few minutes with the rockets on my suit.

I nudged up to the tube and was rewarded with the hollow clink of a magnalock. The line was a good kilometer long, but I could see a tiny shuttlebug start its whirring way up the mooring line, so I'd have fast travel going in. Fully automatic, that response; keyed to the impulse of the magnalock. Gallagher was doing better than might have been expected.

While I waited, I looked over the cargo dumps attached to the other tubes. Nothing but the things we had left, of course. And there was the Antolaric drive—not moored to a tube, but carefully stanchioned directly at the far end of the berg itself, lined up with the balance point of the berg as though it were nudging the glacier from behind.

A pushberger? I asked myself sarcastically. *Is he planning to push the damned berg to the nearest planet? It won't work that way,* I assured myself. *A drive is internal to the ship. Necessarily,* I emphasized warily to myself, but with the haunting feeling that maybe I was missing something, the memory of the *Starfire*'s tuning fresh upon me.

The shuttlebug arrived, and I reached out to grasp the awkward thing, flinging my legs over the upside-down crossbar of the T, and grasping the pipe that led to the tiny foot-long motor firmly clamped to a plastic track along the side of the mooring tube. I nudged the trigger and got the giddy sensation of being thrown forward at nearly half a gee as the tiny electric motor whined along the semigeared track; but the acceleration was brief, and I seemed more to be floating than actually riding as I descended towards the glacier.

It's a funny feeling, watching a glacier come up at you. You're not actually falling toward it, nor it toward you, but it feels like it. All directions are up from the largest object, when you're in a vac suit in space—or even when you're in a small scout. So if you're "up" from the big object and you're approaching it, you're falling—at least in your mind's eye, and it's hard to remember that it's just travel on a straight line.

The glacier "below" me was a spread-out panorama, nearing rapidly, and as it neared I could make out curious black spots. Huge black spots. Faults? No, they were too regular. Paint? Hardly. Probably radiator surfaces. Very probably, from the looks. But how had the man spread radiators directly on an ice surface? And how the devil had one man handled a standard radiator surface at all?

I postponed my curioisity. I'd have at least an hour or so to inspect what had been done while Gallagher made his way around the glacier, and I'd not waste the time.

But as the shuttlebug threw me into deceleration for the landing (and I got the feeling of falling *up*), I saw a suited figure emerge from the bubble dome near the terminus and wave to me.

"Welcome aboard, captain." The voice over the intercom was Gallagher's. Most voices you can't recognize over an intercom, but Gallagher's is different. No intercom can cover that particular tonal quality. How he'd gotten that far that quick I didn't know; but I did know that he was there. Yet—you couldn't even have walked that distance on the skin of a metal ship in a suit with electret shoes, much less on the surface of a glacier with whatever crampers or ice-locks he'd dreamed up to keep him from drifting off the berg.

"Hi," I said weakly. "About ready to give up this foolishness?" It was too late to change my rationale now, though it did sound a little silly, what with the efficiency with which he'd got his stuff secured and gotten ready to go to work.

"I rather thought you'd come because you were ready to give up *your* foolishness," he replied. "Have they got the *Starfire* back to its sluggish norm yet? Independent Spaceways, namely me, can use a good navigator. Glad you're volunteering."

He'd hit the nail on the head about that retuning, and I could feel myself getting red. I was glad I was in a vac suit and he couldn't see it. I kept my voice calm and merely said, "You look to be handling the initial stages okay. But maybe you've had some second thoughts."

I dropped from the shuttlebug. As my feet

touched the ice, I was surprised to find that the electret shoes of my own suit gripped it quite satisfactorily. Somehow I hadn't expected the electrostatic field to work on ice, even though I could see Gallagher standing right there waiting for me with no gripping problem.

He laughed and led me to the bubble dome, and as we unhelmeted in the airlock, I put my foot in my mouth again. "Who's working on the far side of your berg?" I asked. "I saw somebody in a vac suit there as I came in. I thought you were alone."

He didn't answer at once, just opened the inner airlock door. And there, leading off from the far side of the dome, was a yawning shaft going straight down into the ice, with a shuttlebug hanging in its mouth as though it were just as logical to use one inside a ship as out.

"Just me and my bugs, captain," he said grinning.

"Bugs?" I glanced sideways at Gallagher and then back at the hold. Then: "Shuttlebugs I understand. But tunnels like that? Why, it would take a man a month to dig a tunnel like that through a berg like this."

He nodded solemnly. "Aye, and you're right, captain. But I didn't mean just shuttlebugs. Most of the cargo ye landed me here with was bugs of one kind and another." He pointed to a large, odd-looking circular metallic device lying to one side against a wall of the dome. "There's one of the bigger ones there."

I walked over and looked at the thing. It had a rim which I judged would just fit inside the

tunnel; and in the center of the rim a rotating
nose with a screw thread on it. About one turn
every two centimeters, I decided. I looked more
closely at the rim and saw that there were ridges
so that if it were passing through ice it could
slide easily forward, but could not turn readily.
The rim itself seemed to be of two different materials, with a leading edge of metal, and a ten-
centimeter-long trailing section of plastic that
matched the shape, including the grooves.

"Quite a fancy gadget," I said. "But—how
can a thing like this drill through ice? That nose
with the screw thread on it doesn't look very
sharp, and certainly there aren't any teeth
here." I pointed to the surface between the pro-
truding screw nose and the rim.

"Careful. It's hot," Gallagher said—and the
idea of the machine clicked into my mind as an
operating device. The surface was sensibly hot.
The screw would be heated, too; and if you
turned the thing nose-first against a piece of ice
and gave it a shove, it could probably melt its
way rapidly in and then get hold and keep on
going. A sievelike mesh that formed the metallic
surface between the rim and the spinner screw
would take in water, I realized.

"Clever," I said. "Is it self-programming?"

"Pretty much so. It's got maybe the brains of
a mouse. That's what I call it. An ice mouse."

"What does it do with the water?" I asked.

"Just kicks it out the back into the tunnel. I
have to pump it from there. But I've smaller ones
as well, and they make nice little water pipes for
wherever I want to program them to go, so the

pumping's not all that much of a problem."

"And you pump the water out to those radiator surfaces for refreezing?" I asked. "How did you manage to move radiators like that around anyhow? Or, for that matter, where did you get them? I don't recall having landed anything as heavy as a radiator here."

"Well, now. Which question first? The radiators were part of the equipment you landed, believe it or not. But they're not heavy. They're very lightweight plastic, and high-temperature stuff at that. It's amazing how much more heat you can reject at four or five hundred degrees than you can from a low-temperature surface. And since it's the difference you're working with, it makes good sense to have high-temperature radiators where the only energy dumped is by black-box radiation.

"To answer the first question last, though," Gallagher went on, "the water is *not* pumped directly into the radiators. If it were, that's where it would freeze up. Actually, the refrigeration system is a little more complicated than that. But you're right; that water is refrozen after it's pumped where I want it. I scoop it out here and freeze it there. In a few weeks, I'll have this berg balanced out and hollowed out and set up just the way I want it."

I had to admire the system, but I guess I was jealous enough I had to disparage it, too. So, since it was at least chilly if not downright cold in that dome, I shivered as obviously as possible as I said, "It would seem that you've picked a pretty well air-conditioned environment, but aren't you afraid that the constant cold will get to you?"

Gallagher grinned and motioned me to the tunnel leading down. "Come on in," he said. "This dome *is* sort of chilly. It's acting as my airlock right now, but I'll probably replace it with a more conventional airlock sooner or later."

It was a weird sensation, taking a shuttlebug through a tunnel where I could have reached both walls by simply outstretching my arms. The smooth, glistening ridges that had been left behind by Gallagher's ice mouse as it formed the tunnel were as regularly milled and precise as the machine that had made them. But it seemed to me that we'd not gone nearly halfway through when the shuttlebug paused and I swung myself off into a short corridor at right angles.

This one wasn't milled. It wasn't ice, for that matter. And there was proper decking for the soles of my boots to get a better hold. Of course there was no gravity, but I automatically assumed that Gallagher would take care of that—and in the not-too-distant future, at the rate he was going.

"Your hotheaded ice mice," I asked. "Can they be suitably programmed for making the necessary spin-and-balance tubing for a zero M-I spin-grav system?"

"Sure. Ought to have that operating now"— Gallagher glanced at his wrist chronometer— "in another four or five hours. The mice are much busier than I am."

"But with water rushing around in ice tubes,

won't you have some tendency for the tubes to melt and distort?"

"Melt? Sure they will. Except that the water will be brine, and a bit colder than the melting point of ice, so they won't melt very fast. Distort? Well, maybe. Under some conditions of acceleration, the tubes will probably distort a bit, but mostly, since the fluid in the spin tubes goes in one direction and the ship goes in the other, the net friction and thrust is radial to the spin. There shouldn't be much distortion. The tubes will simply gradually work themselves right on out toward the surface. But long before that happens, I'll make a new tube inside. Anything a mouse can do once, he can do all over again. Like I said, they're going to be busier than I am."

"But won't each spin tube leave a hollow place behind it?" I asked.

"Nope. You see right above each spin tube there's a much smaller and much colder tube. So the tubes will plate back on the top what they lose on the bottom."

I paused for a minute and thought that one out. *Up,* of course, was toward the center of the ship, since we were talking about spin gravity. And *down* would be toward the outside of the ship.

"Wait a minute, though. Will that tube on top move out along with the other, larger tube? Or, for that matter, why couldn't you put the cold tube underneath the spin tube to prevent the spin tube from wearing out?"

"One at a time." Gallagher waved me on

through the bulkhead and into a comfortable cabin. "No matter how cold I made the ice, when ice is under pressure, it will melt. Obviously, the spin tubes will be under pressure. Therefore they would gradually melt even if they were kept much colder than would be reasonably efficient. So actually it's much simpler to allow the tube to melt and move itself out, say, three times the distance of its own diameter. Then simply make a new tube in the part it started from. Actually, it'll probably be more complicated that that. There'll be one tube being made and another being filled in while a third, somewhere in between them is operating to keep the spin going."

I could follow that much, but I had a feeling that if I let Gallagher go on, there would be more and more complications added. I could even visualize part of it. The necessary static balance tanks in which the level of water could be changed as other weights—like people—moved around inside the ship and tended to shift the spin-center according to their own positions. But it was really a very standard sort of thing operationally, and I could have drawn a blueprint for it from the memory of my own ship.

"Okay, but just one more point," I finally decided. "This cabin is nice and warm and insulated no doubt. But it *does* have mass and it *will* walk, just like that spin tube. What do you plan to do about that?"

"Now you're getting the picture, Harald!" Gallagher broke into a huge grin. "There's no such thing as static stability in a malleable ship.

And ice is one of the most malleable media you could ask to work with. Actually, this cabin is built with a hot head, something like that the mice use. You turn everything off and let it sink, it would sink right on out through the ice and get spun off into space, once we got spin gravity going. But its rate of sinking won't be very fast, when you consider the square area of floor and the actual mass involved—as a matter of fact, it will float and move toward the inside. But we can do something about it whether it floats or sinks. It's merely a matter of melting a little bit of the ice around the room and then repositioning it by hydrostatic pressure. If I want to move a cabin to the other side of the ship, I can do it in two or three days and scarcely disturb a thing in the process."

I shook my head in awe. The idea of floating cabins around in a ship to make new layouts at will was a bit much for a by-the-book captain and engineer such as myself.

Then Gallagher capped it by summing the whole thing into a nutshell that spelled not only the difference between our ships, but between ourselves and what we represented.

"You see," he said, and his damned voice wasn't even sarcastic, "you're used to thinking in terms of static stability—forms that keep their shape by being rigid; forms that can't change because any major change destroys them.

"My glacier," he went on, and his voice was warm and loving, "she can change and adapt and grow and evolve. She has dynamic stability, and that's quite a different thing."

*   *   *

That Gallagher. I cursed the day I'd met him, as I orbited back to Altura and my spick-and-span ship with all its properly latest gadgets and technological advances incorporated as they were developed. I'd never own my own ship, but by the gods, I told myself, I captained a good one! And when my time was run, as it runs fast in the spaceways, I'd have the cash to buy a small farm and settle down on any planet that I chose where they were accepting colonists.

And there was Gallagher, as though he were mocking me, with an old Antolaric drive and probably the finest engineering talent on the starlanes, using it to make an old hunk of ice into a makeshift ship that would be the laughingstock of the spaceways.

Take those radiator units—made of black plastic which could be turned black side toward the darker portions of space as radiators; or, in event of an emergency, toward the local sun as power collectors. The back surface was a silvery, metalized reflector, air-spaced to insulate the radiators from the icy surface to which they were attached.

And they *were* attached, as were the mooring tubes I'd worried about—quite effectively attached with a gadget he called a hothead bug. It was a combination electric motor with a double-acting screw thread and a very hot nose; similar to his ice mice, but designed as an anchor. Place the thing on the ice and start it moving, it would burrow itself in like a tiny animal; and the screw thread with which it drove itself would remain in the tube behind it, so it could be run in and back out again if you wished. Or it could simply run in pulling a cable behind it and stay there for as long as you liked.

He had small ones for anchoring and big ones —the ice mice—for corridors; and extensive ones with which he was riddling the surface of the ship, creating small-bore tubing in the ice to be used for such things as circulating the cooling brine to maintain the frozen surfaces, and to carry off the melted water to be refrozen where it was needed.

And the drive itself, that I'd seen stanchioned back there like a pushberger. Hell, he'd just positioned it so that the hydrostatic force of its driving would melt it right inside the ship to where he wanted it.

And Gallagher was wasting *that* engineering genius on a hunk of ice! Why, the man could work up to captain, would he abide the rules!

But my own ship didn't look as pretty as she used to look, and though I still saw to it that my men went portside only in threes, I took to going in alone, myself, in full uniform, and be damned to the risk.

The whole thing worried me, and it worried me more as the months passed and the tales began to be traded from bar to bar.

At first Gallagher and his glacier were a roar of laughter that swept the spaceways. But it was more than just a roar of laughter. The spaceways had their first independent shipper, and it was a proud thing, there under the stars.

Overnight there wasn't a man jack on a planet

that wasn't searching for an old Antolaric of his own. But the corporations weren't exactly napping, and they weren't about to let their monopoly of the shipping lanes fall to the tune of secondhand drives. So within days there wasn't an Antolaric to be found that didn't have a company label attached. Though the spaceways had an independent shipper, he was the only one, and it looked like that was sort of permanent; for though the Antolaric is a fairly simple drive to build, it takes power to build the machinery to tool up with. That was where the corporation's monopoly began to show. Outside of corporate hands, power to build machinery was a scarce thing on the planets; Earth had no intention of letting her colonies do more than supply raw materials to her own manufacture.

So, in the long run, there was like to be only the one independent shipper in the starpaths; and though Gallagher and his glacier were a laugh at company expense in any port, the company colonies weren't allowed to trade with him.

How many of the black-market tales were true and how many apocryphal, nobody ever knew. The tales kept running and they grew as such tales will. And one thing was sure: Gallagher had plenty of time and plenty of money these days to satisfy his sociable nature in the bars up and down the spacelanes.

Those tales had the ports and the colonies laughing, but they didn't seem funny to me at all as I sat in my comfortable captain's cabin, with my bright captain's certificate, and wished the man in the netherest regions of hell. Or when I

went into the ports alone for sheer defiance and
came back to my ship unchallenged.

TWO

That was how it was for the better part of two years. The tales told of cargoes that weren't waiting for their normal bidders when the company ships appeared, of how the black market thrived on goods and services they hadn't had before. The tales told of feats of daring and of impossible adventure; and made the company ships a ludicrous caravan of imbeciles, and whether they were believed or whether they were simply recounted for the joy of the telling and hearing was any man's guess.

The tales grew and the laughter grew, and the corporations ignored the laughter, waiting patiently for the original of the tales—the man Gallagher—to make a real wrong move; a move that they could pin him on, but knowing better than to make a martyr of him meantime. Corporations are eternal, while a human has a short span, one lawyer argued. We can wait the upstart out.

But the corporations were smarting for all they pretended to be above the problem; and the colonies were restless, for now the hatred of the colonists for the corporations had a hope to fasten on.

Then Gallagher hit the galactic funny bone with an action as real and as personal as midwifing the birth of a baby, and for the life of me I couldn't see what people found so funny about it. Not funny. Just proud-making in a backward sort of way; and irritating in a much more obvious manner.

It was in a brothel in a port town that this one started.

Now, a man who set out as an independent prospector in the early days could fail and get killed or become a spaceways bum. But for a woman who went with him—or alone—when she failed, or if her man was killed, there was only one place she could wind up. Or if she had too much spunk for the corporation colonies and found herself on the lam—that's where she'd end. It wasn't that the girls were a special class there, but you did find the kind of horse sense that had at least survived in the roughest pioneering man had ever set himself.

So when Gallagher bought out the house and took them all off to a planet of their own, there was sympathy behind the guffaw that went up. And when Gallagher promised them he'd separate the sheep from the wolves along the spaceways bars and bring them a batch of able wolves to help homestead their planet, there wasn't a man who had to be ashamed to volunteer. And after Gallagher had selected the volunteers, there wasn't a man who went but could be proud of being selected.

I had the bad luck to make planetfall where Gallagher was doing his selecting, and I lost an astrogator and a machinist third class to the cause. It made me even madder because underneath I nearly approved of what they were doing.

So I put on my dress uniform and I walked into the port town—too mad to risk driving a skimmer—and I looked up Gallagher where I knew he was to be found—in a bar.

"You got two of my men," I told him without waiting for the amenities.

"Sit down and have a drink," he says. "We'll discuss this polite-like."

I sat down and somehow I didn't seem as little by his side as I had that first day we met. Maybe it was because I'd made the habit of going into ports alone, when it wasn't a secure thing to do. Maybe it was just because I was a captain in the starways, and no matter who owned the ship, I captained her. I'd made that much peace with myself anyhow. But it was an uneasy peace, and I laid it over with a gruffness.

We had a drink and then another before I said my say.

"You're going to pay a price, you know," I told Gallagher, that gruffness ready and waiting for him to upbraid me on the uniform I wore. "The corporations won't let you get away with this forever." It wasn't what I had in mind to say, but it was what came out.

"There's the price of anything," says Gallagher. "And then there's the value. Let's look at the value," he says, "and then we'll discuss the price." The way he said it made sense, and the gruffness began to slip away.

But "Where's the value?" I asked, and knew myself a liar in the asking. "Where's the value?" I heard myself go on. "All you're doing is making yourself the laughingstock of the spaceways."

"Takes a free man to laugh," says Gallagher. "And it takes laughter to make a man free."

We didn't speak again after that, but we kept ordering up the drinks, and first he'd pay the round and then I would. But we didn't speak, and all the time those words of his were echoing back and forth between us, just as if we were saying them over and over to each other.

When I climbed into my bunk that night, the words were still there. "Let's look at the value," the words kept saying, "and then we'll discuss the price." And then, "It takes a free man to laugh, and it takes laughter to set a man free." I kept wondering why I didn't find it funny, what Gallagher was doing; just sad and sort of proud-making in a backward kind of way.

That was that for a long time, and Gallagher was a thorn in the side of the corporations, but not a very big thorn, and they continued to ignore the irritation.

As for Gallagher, he had a thriving colony to ship for now, and the shipping itself was almost more than he could manage with his one glacier. Little by little, the responsibility was beginning to interfere with the habits he preferred, and he was said to complain loudly of the fact.

And me, I listened to the tales that whispered through the bars and knew most of them to be apocryphal but a good part to be true, and I wondered why people found them funny.

I remembered the way the *Starfire* had come to be a thing alive when he had engineered her. How the Port Inspector had ordered the drive reworked to its old condition, the condition-by-the-book, when I'd reached Altura; and how she'd never responded with that particular aliveness again.

I thought of the small farm I'd buy myself when I retired, on a company planet where they'd accept colonists. It looked empty and uninspiring, for I was an old hand at the spaceways now—and old hand by two years—and I'd been aground on corporation planets.

Colonists, you see, weren't exactly indentured slaves, they were just in debt before they left Mother Earth and obliged to work in the company mines or whatever supported the corporation colonies, to pay off the debt. By the books, it took two years to pay off passage to a company planet and another two to earn passage back, if you wanted to go back. The company pay-rates were set accordingly. But meantime you had to live, and the company owned the stores, and your credit was good at the stores. . . .

I had known about colonists, and I had known the conditions under which they lived and worked. Earth is pretty crowded these days, and any chance to get out into opener spaces would be a bargain to some people, I told myself. If I saw things that didn't quite match up to the blurbs and the advertisements that the corporations used to recruit their colonists on Earth, why, a person should investigate, I told myself, before he made a move like that. There will always be people too lazy to find out before they sell themselves into virtual slavery, I told myself. It was no concern of mine.

It hadn't troubled me on my first few runs—at least, I thought it didn't trouble me. It hadn't troubled me the first few times I had to drop crew members into colonies as troublemakers, to join and survive if they could. At least I told myself that didn't trouble me—and truly enough the safety of my ship came first.

Then my schedule called for a stop at Stellamira, to deliver supplies and to pick up a cargo of starstones. It was my second stop at Stellamira. The first time there had been one of my first commissions, and I'd dropped a rebellious crewman there. Stellamira had an unsavory reputation in the starways, but I knew the profits that the corporations made from starstones, and that it was an important colony to them. They were wicked gems, with an hypnotic quality. They were sold and used as tranquilizers. The planet where they were mined was bound to be one of the worst for human life, for it was a new planet, still raw and nearer in time than most to its fiery birth.

I orbited the *Starfire*, let down on the pad at Free Port, and made my way to the company headquarters. Sleek and dry they were, and air conditioned after the heavy humidity of the landing area. Tall, graceful buildings that flanked the edge of the port itself; landscaped and tree-planted and wall-surrounded. They made a striking contrast to the open pits that I had seen scarring the landscape as I came in.

I was welcomed with the quiet hospitality that is accorded rank and shown luxurious quarters. Then I was given a social schedule for the two days I'd be in port that was quite elaborate, and that underscored the need of the local personnel for visiting firemen to entertain them.

But I had seen Gallagher's lander on the port as I came in, and I excused myself from the festivities that first evening early, and headed for the gate that connected Corporation Country to the colonists' area, hoping to find the man. Perhaps it was curiousity, perhaps envy, perhaps simply a need to talk to a fellow from the old country and to hear the brogue again.

I reached the exit and was surprised to find a heavy gate and a guard. I must sign out before leaving. The guard impressed me as a nice, alert young man, but a bit overly concerned for my welfare, since he stressed to me several times that the colonists were a rough lot, and somehow implied without actually saying it that it was beneath the dignity of one of my rank to associate with them.

All in all, I found I'd wasted a good fifteen minutes, yattering back and forth with the guard, and still not gotten anywhere toward signing out, when one of the men who had officially greeted me on arrival showed up.

"We're sorry our company displeases you," he opened. "We've usually quite sufficient entertainment for visitors of your rank." He nodded back toward the building. "Is there perhaps something missing? Or possibly," he added with a leering twinkle, "you'd like me to recommend? If you're after rather . . . bawdy entertainment, there's Suzie's. Her place is just inside the colonists' area and is set up for the entertainment of ship's officers as well as crew. Suppose I escort you."

I smiled at him, rather grimly. It was on the tip of my tongue to say I'd seen Gallagher's lander and wanted to see if I could locate Gallagher himself, but something warned me against it. Instead I merely said, "I've a curiosity about the colonists . . ." and left the sentence hanging there.

"Oh?" His face looked grimmer yet. "Then," he said, "I shall insist upon sending along an escort, though I shall not volunteer myself. We do have a bit of trouble now and then. And . . ."

I drew myself up. Though I'm not tall, I do command a ship and can adopt the manner of authority necessary to such a command when it is required, whether with equals or subordinates. "I think that I am quite capable of managing myself, even"—I added to appease his apparent concern—"among rabble. And I am not unarmed," I added, lightly touching the laser gun at my hip.

With that I turned and strode through the gate, nor did I bother to sign the chit of paper on the guard's desk. I simply turned my back on the two of them and walked through, seething a bit inside at the necessity to pull rank to do as I pleased in a free port.

Just beyond the gate I found myself quickly submerged in a surge of pleasure-seeking humanity. On my right was Suzie's Place, proclaiming itself with neon lights and a rather luxurious entrance. Beside the entrance was a small sign; *Corporation and Off-Planet Personnel Only*. It rather startled me, and I looked at it again to make sure I'd read it right, but it remained, innocuously unobtrusive, but unmistakably adamant.

I shrugged and looked around. Opposite and beyond were hucksters and bazaars and shops, grocers and the like. Much the same as you will see in any of the free ports of space, I decided, and probably not one whit rougher. Not only because of the sign, but because the executive had suggested it, I ignored Suzie's Place, which looked much the most inviting of the honky-tonks, and made my way around the corner.

The crowd was thick and noisy, yet I noticed people shrugging away from close contact with the uniform I wore—an odd reaction, since in most free ports a captain's uniform is a prime target for all the peddlers and vendors of this and that who hope to fast-talk a buck out of any rank they see.

I made my way past Suzie's and rounded the corner to find a less luxurious side to the same building, and centered in it a set of old-fashioned swinging doors that spoke a time-honored language meaning *bar,* though they were probably copied out of an old Earth Western. By their sides was a small, again innocuous-looking sign that read *Colonists*.

This was still the Suzie's that I'd been told to visit; yet it was a different Suzie's than the entrance nearest the gate. I was tempted to turn back entirely. The dirt, the noise and smell and perhaps the crowds that inexplicably shrugged away from me instead of ganging to sell me wares had weakened my decision. Actually I wanted to go back to the cleaner atmosphere, to the quiet, to the—the womb of my own kind. Instead I turned to the swinging doors.

As I started to push my way through, I met resistance, and looked up to see a tall, bearded fellow staring at me over the doors.

"S'matter, sonny?" he said belligerently. "Can't you read?"

"I beg your pardon?" I said formally, and stepped a half pace backward, simultaneously tugging the door out from in front of the bearded man who had been pushing to hold it shut. My action caught him by surprise, and he came tumbling out. With a sidestep and a push at his back as he went by, I managed not only to get through the door, but to leave him sliding into the dirt outside.

That immediate arrogance, I decided as I walked in, might have been a mistake, though I'd not have changed it if I could. It was a long barroom, with tables and bar stools crowded and standees to boot. A hush came over its entire length. Every eye was on the door and on me as I strode through. Figures at various tables began slowly rising to their feet, and I was debating whether to stand where the wall beside the door would still shelter my back, or whether to continue my firm stride forward, when a voice bellowed over the crowd.

"Ho! It's Captain Dundee of the *Starfire*.

Harald, will ye join me for a drink?"

There was Gallagher, seated with a woman and two men at a table near the far end of the room.

Hands loose at my sides and ready, though with no gesture to indicate that I recognized the hostility around me, I made my way straight to his table and saw, from the corner of my eye, the men who had started to rise slowly sinking back into their chairs. As I approached, the two men who had been seated with Gallagher rose and left; and Gallagher waved me to join him and the tall, rather hawk-faced woman beside him. It wasn't really a hawk face, I realized as Gallagher rose to introduce us. The nose was decided, the chin firm, but not excessively so. It was the intensity of the face that gave it that appearance. And the eyes. They were eyes that saw what they looked at: deep, interested eyes.

"Suzie," said Gallagher, "this is Harald Dundee."

She smiled and her whole face was smiling. Suzie? I was astonished. This was Suzie's Place. A place of entertainment is the euphemism, although it's an exact statement. Bar, music, dancing, gambling and girls downstairs; bedrooms upstairs, obviously. And Suzie its mistress. But she didn't have the blowsy look. And she was dressed in slacks. A red shirt. Tight black slacks. Makeup, but not much.

"How do you do," I said. It seemed rather inadequate. I was surprised to meet a woman who was a person in that role, and I don't think I hid it well.

We were interrupted at that point, which was

probably just as well. The murmur and background buzz in the room had been taking up where it had left off, but now it died abruptly, and Suzie, Gallagher and I all looked around to see the bearded man standing in the door looking around for me. He spotted me as quickly as I spotted him, and headed toward me, then noticed who I was with, hesitated, and came forward again.

I wasn't exactly spoiling for a fight, but he looked as though he were, and I was relaxing my tensing muscles to be ready. His belligerence faded as he approached, but he came with obvious purpose.

"Come join us, Seth," Gallagher invited as he got near enough to hear. "This is Harald Dundee, captain of the *Starfire*. Seth Thompson, Harald," he added.

The man extended his hand and I reached out to grasp it until I realized the gesture was not one of greeting. He spread the fingers wide, and two were missing. "We've met," he said shortly. "In an engine room."

And I remembered. I hadn't recognized him through the beard, but I did now. A burly giant, slow of speech but strong. It had been a brawl in the engine room, and it had been this man who had swung a wrench at me. I'd really had no reason to have been there, as far as I knew then; the fight had been between two ratings, and I had thought that I'd only happened to be passing in the corridor outside. When I'd stepped through the bulkhead to see what was going on, I'd seen nothing but a hand and a wrench, swinging toward my skull.

My reactions had been fast then, too. I'd stepped back and slammed the bulkhead door. It hadn't closed completely, and it hadn't blocked off the scream, but when I'd opened the door again there was no fight and no one around. Only a trail of blood. He had gone to the medic, but he had claimed an injury on duty and something about a wrench slipping from his fingers and getting caught in some machinery, so I could have dropped it there. But I hadn't. I'd had him jailed, and when we'd landed at Stellamira, I'd had him dropped off.

Not satisfied with that, I'd let the other engineer ratings go, one by one. A captain may not always know what goes on in the minds of the crew, I'd told myself, but he can be fairly sure that when he walks into a setup like that, there was something cooking that wasn't good. So I'd blacklisted them, every one, when I bounced them off my ship. A hard policy, perhaps, but one according to the books.

Gallagher was waiting silently. "We've met," I agreed shortly.

The face had scars that hadn't been there before, and it was working now in a controlled anger that I could well understand, whether I could agree with it or not. Gallagher was silent, and I stayed silent, too, watching that face working, watching the anger of the man, and wondering what the odds were if it came to blows again. There was Gallagher—and Suzie—and the rest of the barroom. All unknowns and too many unknowns. Even if it were just the two of us, it was his size, his strength, his nearly berserk anger, if it broke, against my quickness.

I kept myself relaxed. It's fatal to tense before any first move. But I was ready. Seth is slow to react. It was probably several seconds—maybe as many as fifteen.

Then his face began contorting, and that I couldn't read at all. I just stood loose and ready. Then words began to come out and I relaxed. A man like that will talk or fight, but not both.

The words were slow and halting, and they came past a heavy barrier of emotion. "You're here now, captain," he said, and his tone was ugly but the decision had been made and I could listen more and watch less. "In my world. I think I want to show you what you dropped me into when you dropped me here, blacklisted so I had no way off."

Then quite suddenly the face broke into a grin that was more weird than the anger that had preceded it. The anger was gone. The man turned to Gallagher almost happily. "The captain had good reason to drop me," he said, the words still coming as slow as the man's thinking processes. "We wanted his ship. He was young and we thought we could get it. Then we'd have been real free men in space, like you are, Dublin."

At that he paused again, and his face contorted with thought. "Only we'd have been pirates, not like you," he said, and the honesty of the man had me on his side completely.

There was a long pause, and nobody spoke at all. I could feel Gallagher and Suzie waiting, and

I was waiting and almost wondering what was coming. It was like losing your balance on a precipice and catching it again. You just wait a second, not really thinking.

The big bearded face turned back to me, and it held a new, a rather surprised expression. "You lived and kept your ship," he said, "no thanks to me. But I lived, and that's no thanks to you. Now you come with me. I'm going to show you how I lived. I've waited to find you again, just once. I was going to kill you when I did. But I reckon," and his head swung back and forth between the three of us, "that Gallagher and Suzie have made a difference in me. They've made a difference to all of us. And now I'm just going to show you."

The man was deadly serious, and I would refuse him at cost. What that cost would be I could only guess. I looked at Gallagher and I saw a sort of proud expression on his face, like you get when your dog recognizes your needs as well as his own. And Suzie had a funny, happy sort of look.

Seth must have hated me, completely and absolutely. For how long? Two years? Then I realized it must have been more than just hatred. It was an anger and hatred so deep that it probably kept him alive. He had to live for the privilege of killing me someday.

This was the someday. The day for which he had lived through hell and all the degradations that hell had presented. Yet he was foregoing his day in some queer reasoning that had to do with Gallagher and Suzie.

I looked at them, each of them in turn, and the proud look they had. Then Gallagher nodded at me and turned to Seth.

"Sounds like a fair proposition to me, Seth," he said genially. "A good look at Stellamira should be a part of any captain's education. But if you don't mind, I think I'll be coming along. I think I want the captain to see what's here; but I think, too, I want to be sure he gets back in one piece. He'll be a good witness . . . later."

I didn't know what he meant, but I didn't really care. I knew damned well I had little choice in the matter. You don't deny a man when he's paid the price that Seth had paid . . . and there was Gallagher again, back then, not now, saying it again in my mind. "There's the price of anything, and then there's the value. Let's look at the value, and then we'll discuss the price."

Suzie was rising from her seat. "I'm going too," she said, which surprised me. That was the second time, and it never did end. Suzie has never failed to surprise me, and I guess she never will. She just doesn't fit any pattern I've ever known. Suzie is . . . well, Suzie.

That night my senses were shocked as they had never been before. The conditions under which the colonists on Stellamira lived were unbelievable. Cattle are better cared for.

It's a sterile planet: hot to the edge of the degree that a man can stand, and not evolved to the point of life in sea or on land, which meant that, although the atmosphere was adequate for a human, everything else had to be imported.

That first area was the "pleasure" area: the free port proper. Crowded, noisy, dirty, bawdy, horrible, but livable, if you could call that living. But then you came to the living area, and it wasn't fit for beasts. The stench itself was enough to make you ill. The quarters were ramshackle huts. The streets were dirt and filthy. The faces of the people—and people were everywhere, crowded into a small area—were haggard and hopeless.

"But why don't they build themselves better quarters?" I asked aghast. "There's rock, if nothing else, for building . . ."

"If you want to eat, you work. If you work, you work fourteen hours a day. There's not enough water, not enough food, and you work for both of them. From the time you're eight or ten years old," Seth said. "Mining can be done pretty early."

Then there were the mines themselves. As he had said, men, women, and children working them. I shan't try to describe the mines—I wish I could forget them.

Starstones are a major product commercially, and there were rare minerals as well. Which meant that the mining of the planet was invaluable. But it takes a lot of mining to make a cargo worth carrying through the spaceways. The mining left no time for comfort or the building of luxuries such as proper living quarters.

And there was no escape. You can't escape into a planet that's as inhospitable as Stellamira and survive. As to saving and buying passage back? I found the answer to that one, too. The company couldn't afford to have eyewitnesses returning to Earth. If you scrimped and saved and starved to keep the "pay" that the company provided, it was stolen from you in the long run. There was one other choice than putting up with it. That was suicide, and I gathered that the suicide rate on Stellamira was as high as you get anywhere.

It was a stinking, sweating, slave-labor life, with the honky-tonk of a free port the only luxury to be had. Not enough water. Not enough food. Too much work. And right in front of their eyes the company executives living in luxury.

No wonder the company kept the ships' officers in its own compound and guarded that compound. No wonder the company men went armed to the teeth. No wonder the canaille—the colonists—were feared and hated in company quarters. No wonder you ran the risk of murder and sudden death coming among the colonists, if you were of the ranking company personnel. Those colonists had been tempted here with promises of wealth. "Free men," the company would tell you. Free to go anywhere on the planet they wanted to—if there were anywhere a man could go and live. Free to work for the company or not work for it—and starve. Free to leave when they liked—if they could pay passage. Free to die. Yes, that freedom they had.

By the time I said good-bye to Gallagher and Seth and Suzie, I was boiling mad. I had promised myself that a report on this planet and the conditions it supported would go straight to the U.N. Space Commission.

Gallagher laughed when I told him that. Seth snorted, but he seemed more eager for it to happen. Suzie just shrugged.

I asked Gallagher why he laughed.

"The Space Commission?" he asked. "You can rub their noses in it for a bit, perhaps. Might even get some results, for they do manage to look away mostly; but this stink is enough to get up a nose that's forced to smell it. In the long run it'll do ye nae gud," he said, lapsing into the brogue.

"Aye, but I'll only be starting there," I told him. Then, brusquely, "I'll carry it as far as it must go. To the news media . . ."

"The controlled press?" Gallagher laughed heartily this time. Then he sobered. "You're a young man, Harald," he said, "with still an ideal or two left under that uniform, and a lot to learn. It won't hurt you to try. Oh," he added, "there'll be times, if you try, when it will hurt the bejesus out of the seat of your pants, which is a euphemism for where you wear your stripes; but it will do your ever-living soul a pile of good. So I wish you well."

But Seth was grimly satisfied. "You dropped me off here, captain," he said, in his slow voice, "to live or die, and I don't really think now you knew what you were condemning me to. If you should report this to the Space Commission, we'll consider old scores settled."

"It's not for that I'd be doing it," I told him with a grin, matching the pace of his speech. "But you're right. I'd no idea that I was condemning you to *this*. This," I said grandly, waving my hand to indicate the entire habited and habitable part of the planet, "is beneath the dignity of the human race and must not be allowed to continue." I had faith in my captain's stars in those days, that I'd be heard. I headed back to the company compound head high, chin out, ready to administer to rank what I'd administered in my time to file.

There was no trouble at all in returning to the corporation compound. The guard nodded me cheerfully in, and as I entered the lobby of the main building, I found the exec who'd seen me out with such concern wandering about as though he'd just arisen from a refreshing night's sleep.

"Ho, captain," he said. "Did you enjoy your night among the canaille?"

My eyes glinted hard. "Canaille, is it?" I asked. "They looked like human beings to me. Human beings enslaved and degraded." At that point the liquor I'd been imbibing with Gallagher must have got my tongue, for I went on in the fury that was seething within me. "This planet is a disgrace to the starways," I said, "and the U.N. Space Commission will hear about it, in detail, when I return."

His eyebrows went up then, and the sarcasm was light in his voice. "Oh? The good captain was displeased?" It was a soft voice, and it stung to the heart of my disgust.

I described with great accuracy and detail just exactly what I had seen, and I quoted the laws on the Space Agency books that protected colonists from just this treatment. My tongue was loose and ready, and I described not only what I had seen, but the detail of my plans for presenting the problem on Earth, not just to the Space Commission, but to the news media—the underground and the overground media; for if I got a hearing in the more-or-less black-market news area, the overground media could not ignore the problem.

He listened, and he must have questioned me in that light, faintly sarcastic tone, for some time. If I'd been less sure of the privileges of rank, or had taken a better look at the consequences to him and his ilk of my doing what I was saying, perhaps I'd have been more careful. Perhaps. But my tongue was loosened and my confidence long.

It's hard for a young man to realize what a man will do to a man; and even when he sees it happening to others, the security in which he was born and raised has buffered him about with the indifferent armor of knowing it can't happen to him. It never occurred to me that it could happen to me.

I went to my luxurious quarters, slipped out of my jacket and sidearm; but instead of going to bed, I got out paper and pen and began to draft a report on Stellamira. It was a violently worded start, though I was trying my best to couch the violence I felt in the formal terms necessary.

When a knock came at the door, I opened it without hesitation. It was a three-guard on the threshold, and the rating in charge said simply, "Come with us, captain."

"Who's called for me?" I asked, my naïveté

still self-assured and confidently unalert.

"The brass wants to talk to you," said the rating with what I took to be unintended brusqueness.

". . . wants to talk to you, *sir*," I said. Ratings must be taught from the start.

He looked at me startled, caught my eye, dropped his. "*Sir,*" he said sullenly. "The orders are immediately and as you are."

Now, a rating cannot question his orders, and though I was in no mood to talk to anyone, I wasn't sleepy either. Perhaps, I decided, I *was* in a mood to talk to someone in authority. Perhaps I could get some action immediately, even ameliorate conditions so that I could tone down my report. I followed the guard.

A ground car took us through the gate into the port part of the colonists' area, through it to its outskirts, and pulled up before the local gendarmerie.

"Are your officers *here?*" I asked in surprise, still unsuspicious.

"This is the place they said," the flunky replied without any form of respect again, but I ignored it this time and went in without protest . . .

. . . and found myself bustled into a cell by armed company police.

Prison? *I* was a prisoner. And all the shouts for information, all the shaking of the bars that my fury indulged in, were to no avail. What the future held I could only guess, at least for what seemed forever, before the colony manager finally appeared. Then I wished I didn't know.

"You think you could get away with something like that?" he asked without preliminary. A hard-eyed little man with a face like a weasel and deep circles under his eyes, gray lids drooping over them.

"And just what charges do you think you're holding me on?" I asked in turn, cold with helplessness, the fury bottled. "Your Earth managers will hear of this."

"My orders are standing, direct from *your* Earth managers, mister," he said. "Direct. With details of what to do. They don't name you except as John Doe, but they apply. They're . . ."

"To let me out of here immediately," I said furiously, but with a hollow in the pit of my stomach.

"Oh, yes," he said, and the weasel face grimaced. "Oh, yes indeed. Almost immediately. We just put you here temporarily. Easier that way." He stopped then, deliberately, and stood there watching me. I could feel myself shaking, and I tried to control the shakes. I hoped he couldn't see them.

But the crooked grin told me he had seen, and translated to his pleasure, and I knew him for a sadist.

"The doctor'll be here to examine you tomorrow," he said slowly, taking his time to refine my reactions. "You'll go to the psych ward. Obviously insane, you know. Probably dangerous. Certainly dangerous to your ship and crew."

Then his voice grew hard and ugly. "After a few doses of shock therapy," he said, with a yearning in his voice under the hardness, "you'll

be amenable. Quite amenable. Amenable
enough to ship back to Earth. You'll be cared for
the rest of your life, so you needn't worry."

Then abruptly he grinned, and there was a
pleasure in that grin that watered my knees. "I'll
be there, watching you," he said.

I'd read about a sadist's grin, but I'd never
seen it. You can't describe it. It's—you're the
bug looking up at the boy sticking a pin through
you to pin you to a paper. . . .

He left then, and the barred door at the end of
the corridor outside my cell clanged shut. Then
a bolt clicked. It was the most final sound in the
universe.

Time stopped. It just stopped. There's no feeling like it. It could have been hours or days or
minutes or years. The light filtering through the
high, barred window didn't change, so intellectually I knew that no time had passed. But I
knew it internally even more so, with a deep,
endless knowledge that went on and on and
on. . . .

THREE

How long it was by a clock before I pulled myself together, I don't know. The light from the window hadn't changed, but eternities had passed.

Then I began to explore that cell, looking for a way out. Every crack in the paint, every scratch on the wall, every corner, every seam where floor met wall or wall met ceiling. Given a reason for doing so, I think I could probably give you a microscopic description of that little company jail cell.

And the jailhouse. I set myself to recall every detail I'd seen. It was a small building, all ground-floor level, located at the brow of a steep hill. I pulled myself up to the window. The hill fell away abruptly with tumbled boulders.

Solidly built, that jailhouse. Not the flimsy construction of most of the colony. The way that jail was built tells the story of the corporation colonies. It wasn't built to permit escape.

It was with a feeling of hopelessness buried as deeply as I could bury it; and a stubborn optimism that I set firmly on top of the hopelessness, that I started to work on the only plan I could dream up.

I scraped up all the grit and dust there was on the floor of that cell—and there was dust and grit, though it seemed all too clean to me— trying to gather a pile. Then I took my shoelaces, the best grinding surfaces I had, and I worked the heaviest grit onto the shoelaces, and I hooked them around the bars of the window and began grinding, back and forth, back and forth, reaching above my head and working with a ferocity that took little heed of blood-drained, aching arms and numb fingers, rubbing and rubbing and rubbing—trying to make that dirt act as a grinding agent.

I wasn't making much progress, but I was doing the only thing I could dream up to do. I couldn't just stay there waiting to be made into a vegetable.

The first shoelace was beginning to fray, and it had been pitch-dark outside for eternities, when there was a quiet laugh above my head, and I heard the lightest of whispers. "Leave it, captain. Let me give it a try."

It was only minutes, then, before the bars began to slide out of sight, one at a time, neatly cut. I didn't know how he cut them, and I still don't. I didn't care. The hand that stuck in the window and beckoned, holding the last bar, was the gladdest sight I've ever seen. I didn't waste time, and I didn't make a sound, hoisting myself to that window, sliding my head and shoulders out.

The figure beyond was holding the edge of the window and leaning aside to give me room to join him on—of all things—a short mooring tube. A plastic, expandable bourdon mooring tube—the type used in space to keep things from drifting into or away from your ship. Just big enough for one man to hang onto with a rope harness, and the tube stretched above our heads as well as down.

The figure was clinging to the tube with a regular climbing belt, but there were no spikes on his shoes—that would have been fatal to the structure itself. Instead, I could see dimly that a loose lacework of rope had been draped over the tube providing foot and hand grips for its climber.

"Climb on down, captain," the figure whispered. "I'll be with you in a minute." Then he clung to the window while I made my way down the rope network.

When I reached the ground and let go, I stumbled, then got to my feet and looked back up. He'd leaned back on his belt and was seaming those bars back in so that the method of my escape would not become immediately apparent.

I stood at the bottom of the tube looking up, trying to see what he was doing, when another soft whisper reached me. "This way. Quickly, captain."

It's hard to tell, on a barely moonlit slope, when someone whispers, where they are or what they are. I looked around, my eyes adjusting, and could make out two figures working on some equipment. Then the tube behind me began hissing down, and the man who'd cut the bars was beside me as it flattened to the ground. He ignored me and began strapping the collapsed tube together, while the other two began detaching what must have been a compressor from the lead-ins.

But a fourth figure was tugging at my sleeve, and I turned and followed it down a steep way through the boulders to a point where we reached a rock wall behind some buildings. We jumped down from the rock wall, and I could just make out a skimmer there, in an angle behind one building and an alley just beyond.

"Hadn't I better help with the equipment?" I whispered.

The figure shook its head. "No. Gallagher's waiting." I realized then for the first time that it was a girl beside me, and then that it was Suzie. "Get those clothes off and put these on," she said. "We may need a captain's uniform someday."

I took the clothes she shoved into my arms and looked around for a place to undress. She giggled, then whispered fiercely, "Right here. Right now. And fast! We need those clothes, you need these, and there's not much time."

I did as she said, though my modesty hurt me, and as I stopped at the skivvies, she gestured those off, too, and I obeyed. While I was naked as a jay, the first of the men landed beside me, reached back, and was handed the heavy equipment. Then the other two landed and started manhandling it into the back door of the building.

As the packaged mooring tube went past, Suzie shoved my uniform, shoes, and skivvies on top, and they were taken in, too.

I had a bit of trouble with the garb she had handed me in the dark, but I got on the old pants and shirt and a kind of sweatshirt affair—not too clean, I judged from the odor—and a pair of sandals. I glanced at the legend painted on the door that had closed behind my benefactors, and could just make out in the dim scatterlight: *Surplus Sales.*

As I was buckling on the sandals, Suzie leaned forward and passed something damp across my face and hair. Damp and slightly sticky. "Have you ever been an actor?" she whispered.

I had been taken by surprise by the physical contact and started to reach up to feel my face, but she grabbed my arms and said, "Wait a minute till it dries." Even as she spoke I could feel the damp sticky stuff cooling and hardening.

"I . . . uh . . . no, I've never tried acting," I stammered.

"Well, that's okay. It won't take much. Come on." She went to the skimmer, opened the door and gestured me in. I saw Seth at the controls as I bent to enter. Then I felt a light tap on the back of my neck . . .

. . . and came to, knowing I was on a ship in orbit. My head was throbbing, and I hadn't opened my eyes, but I knew I was in orbit by the . . . more a feel than anything else that orbit gives you, but I suppose it's compounded of various feels. The coriolis of the spin-grav, so different from planet gravity. The feel of the ship. The quality of vibration. I'd spent too many hours with them not to recognize them.

I opened my eyes and knew I was in the control cabin of Gallagher's *Glacier*. There could be no control cabin quite like it, of course. Any normal ship, you might have to guess; but Gallagher's control cabin is hand-rigged, and though it's neither haywire nor breadboarded, there's an unfinished quality about the consoles and other formalized controls that no manufacturer would tolerate, though the wiring itself is something ships' engineers dream of.

I was in the navigator's chair, tilted back for acceleration and/or comfortable sleeping. There was no one at the controls, so we were on automatics. I located Gallagher himself when I sat up and looked around, in the tiny galley that opened off the control room, whistling cheerfully under his breath.

The stiffness I half-expected either evaporated or wasn't there as I stood groggily. The throbbing in my head disappeared. My face, though, felt stiff, and when I reached my hand to it, a tiny fleck of blood came off.

"Go wash your face," Gallagher greeted me cheerfully. "You're not dead yet."

He gestured toward a small 'fresher next to the galley, and I looked in the mirror there. My face and hair were covered with blood. I looked like I'd just been murdered, or just committed one. Synthablood, I realized, remembering the damp, sticky stuff, and I began dousing water over my face. I needed that for more than the synthablood. I needed to bring myself out of the grogginess. I started out being careful not to splash water on my clothes, then noticed the old sweatshirt affair I was wearing, dirty and fairly smelly, and didn't bother.

I was mopping up with a towel when I looked up to see Gallagher lounging in the bulkhead, grinning. "You've changed some, formerly dapper captain," he said happily.

"I've been in some changing places," I noted, and found myself grinning back, though I couldn't decide why I felt quite so happy. There were enough problems I could see ahead to keep a man worried, like getting my lander and the men in it back from the planet, and getting the *Starfire* to Earth so I could report the renegade Stellamira Company. I was out of the trap now that would have prevented it, and I must needs get on with the job.

"Who were those people who sprung me out of the clink?" I asked. "Suzie was with them."

"Suzie and her crew? Well, you could say she was with them. It's her gang. They're what you might call a corporate underground. They do me a bit of a favor now and then—like getting you out of the clink—and I managed to return the favor now and again."

"Well," I said carefully, "I owe them somewhat more than a favor. But I plan to report the Stellamira Company to the U.N. Space Commission and change conditions there. Perhaps that will do a bit toward evening the score. Do you know what those company bastards had rigged for me?"

"I've a pretty good idea." Gallagher was looking at me in a skeptical way, but his voice went hard at this, with a fury under it. "I've seen some of their results. That's what Suzie and I were sort of planning to change. And I don't think we can wait for you to report to the Space Commission, Harald. Springing you is going to make things pretty hot down there."

"Oh?" I was concerned. "But how can you— and Suzie—change it? It will have to be reported, of course. But perhaps, if I can be of assistance in ameliorating conditions meanwhile— I certainly owe them anything I can do. She's an odd one to be mixed up in something like that."

Gallagher's skeptical look changed to one of amusement. "Suzie? Yep. An odd one, you might rightly say. Never quite met anyone like her for guts or brains or practical ability. She runs that place of hers like a stage manager, and besides what comes to the house itself, she's rumored to have slept personally with half the guys on the planet, corporate *and* private. I think she does it for fun as well as for purpose, though I think purpose would be sufficient motive. She knows what she wants to accomplish, and that's the best way to do it. The girls she takes in are her kind: they're doing what they're doing because they're bachelor types with a goal in mind. If they're not that type, they don't get into Suzie's. They're the only ones on the planet with freedom to organize what needs organizing and the ability to do it, too. But even if they have the goals she has, a gal can't come in unless she has that bachelor attitude, which," he finished dryly, "is somewhat different than what you find in a normal house."

I looked at him, puzzled, but I changed the

subject. "What did she hit me with?" I asked, rubbing the lump at the back of my neck. "And why?"

Gallagher chuckled. "I reckon she didn't know whether you could handle a bit part as a quick study, so she had to make you into the one kind of actor who can't go up on his lines. She and Seth got you onto the landing field as a drunken crewman who had had one too many. The guards all frequent the place, too, and if Suzie says 'jump', they jump. She knows too much about each of them personally for them to question her, even on Stellamira. As for your other question—what she hit you with—why, I imagine she used a little syrette known as a roller's tap. Good for using on drunks, whether you want to roll 'em or not, and not particularly harmful, if you don't mind a long sleep.

I was clean now—that is, my face and hair. My clothes still stank. I'd been standing there, listening to Gallagher with both ears and not particularly noticing a tugging at my senses until it had been going on, probably for some time. Now the tugging finally got my attention, and I noticed that the feel of the ship was somehow wrong.

Automatically my mind slipped into what I think of as *captain's gear,* and I began paying attention to the details of the feel of the ship. The gravity was wrong. Instead of the smooth spin that one should feel in orbit with a slight coriolis displacement that spacemen automatically compensate for but never quite get used to, there was a quiver.

I listened for the throb of motors, and I heard it, just barely. I listened with each of my other senses in turn, but it was only the two—that little balance point between my ears that said something was wrong with the gravity and that faint quiver.

"Dublin," I said, "there's something out of kilter with—I think your gravity control, though it might be more serious."

He nodded slowly. "Thought you might notice, Harald." His tone was satisfied. "You're not all by-the-book, I guess—there's a little seat-of-the-pants left in you. Yep. The gravity's a bit out of kilter. Catewampus, you might call it. We're enlarging the hull, making holds for a cargo of about five thousand people. You better begin getting familiar with the ship, anyhow, so come along. I'll show you."

That "five thousand people" should have alerted me, but it didn't. I wanted to see that ship, and the reason for looking was immaterial at the time. Gallagher headed through the bulkhead at the back of the control room, and I followed.

We stepped into what should have been a straight, simple corridor—tunnel would be a better word—and I recognized the handiwork of his mice. But it wasn't straight and it wasn't simple. It was bent and twisted like a child's jump rope that had been dropped to lie as it fell, twisted and turned, with bumps and slopes and curves. It was a crazy child's toy of a corridor, and I sucked in my breath, thinking that those bumps might be leaking; but Gallagher just stepped out along it like it was the normal way to build a corridor.

It was even more of a shock when we reached the first of the engine rooms. This room contained a rather king-sized power converter unit, about four meters long and a good one and a half meters in diameter. The thing was nosed over at the heavier end, all out of level in respect to the servicing catwalk next to it; and there was a thin trickle of water seeping out from in front of the contact surface that was swept up by a pump and circulated, presumably to a better location.

I stood and stared. Then I found my voice. "Why in hell did you install it that way?"

"Didn't," said Gallagher. "It crept."

I stared at him in amazement, and he began to explain, almost sheepishly. "Ever hang a weight by a string tied around a cake of ice? The string will melt through the ice, but the cake of ice will stay whole. The ice welds itself together behind the string. Well," he went on, sort of chuckling under that sheepish look, "this ship. Her parts and specifications creep and move around like she was digesting 'em. I reckon I spend more time reorienting machines and chambers than I did building her in the first place. But she keeps ahead of me and has 'em screwed up most of the time. It's kind of a family battle, you might say."

I looked at the cold ice, melting against the converter unit, and I listened to the warmth of his voice as he spoke of *her*, and at that she seemed warmer to me. Like a man invites you into his home and there's his crazy-quilt wife, and you're startled at first. But there's a love be-

tween them, and before you leave, you realize
she's warm and comfortable and loving and
more beautiful because of it than the dolls you
normally meet.

But I couldn't think of anything to say, so
"Plastic flow?" I asked.

"Yep."

"But how do you compensate?"

"Nope," he answered. "Compensate's not the
right word. Rebuild's more like it. We expand or
shrink or change as a constant and according to
circumstances. You get used to change as your
only constant after a while," he said tolerantly,
and reached out and touched a switch, but nothing particular seemed to happen as he went on.
"In general, anything that has to be moved
rapidly I've coupled with the proper type heat-
ing surfaces and hotheads so that it can be done
fast. Like this one," he said as the converter unit
began tilting very slowly and moving back into a
level position. The little pump that had been taking water from the melting ice in front of the unit
began taking considerably more water as the
unit realigned.

"Things like the corridor we just came
through—well, they're not too essential, so I just
wait until they get reasonably uncomfortable
before I bore a new one and fill in the old one."

"But if the converter—" I was worried. A
catewampus converter is somewhat to worry a
man—"if the converter keeps doing this, then
everything in the ship must move around or float
around or . . ."

Gallagher guffawed, and his laugh echoed and

tinkled in that ice cavern. Finally, "Well, yes and no," he said. "The cabins and things float, and like I showed you back when you first came aboard while I was building her, I just melt water from behind them and pump it under pressure in front of them, and squeeze them back into place. But she does have one habit that's harder to manage. She expands radially, leaving a hollow in the center. And boy, does she get fat! Then I have to really go to work. Put a plastic skin over her, melt the outside, and pump it back inside. Five times out is about as big as I can let her expand and still keep her in kilter before I have to pause and shrink her back down —put her back on a diet, so to speak. But this time I'm ballooning her on purpose. That's what we're doing now. Giving her a bigger belly so we'll have room for the people."

"What people?" I asked, though I was beginning to get an idea of what he had in mind.

"The people of Stellamira, of course," he said in surprise. "You saw how rough it was there before. Well, it's twice as rough today, on account of your escape. We weren't planning this for another three months, but I reckon the deadline's sort of called."

"But—but Dublin! I'm going to report it to the Space Commission. It will be . . ."

"Sometimes," he interrupted, "I get to thinking you've got right good sense underneath all that company learning of yours. But other times," he went on, keeping me from speaking, "I get despairing of you. Just how are you planning to get to Earth to report the 'situation,' as you call it, even if that would do any good?"

"Why, the *Starfire* . . ."

"The *Starfire* took off pretty near twelve hours ago. While you were in prison. In command of her executive officer, and with word that you'd been taken space-hazy and were confined to hospital on Stellamira. They were planning to send you back on the next ship through, and you'd have been space nuts all right by then. Real nuts."

"But—spacemen only go space-hazy after . . . the sort of accident that leaves them in a suit too long, or . . . or . . ."

Gallagher looked at me kindly. "Space nuts," he said softly, "is a disease that is manufactured in the psych wards, and only there. It is a convenient way to get rid of a man, and it's never been and never will be a real hazard of real space. Not the symptoms and the effects that you see when you see the 'victims' they'll show you. The vegetables. A guy can go space nuts in a suit —temporary insanity—and get over it. What they call the space-psycho is the one they manufacture. You were supposed to be it. Now," he said, dropping the subject as though it were completed to anyone's satisfaction, "you are, like it or not, stuck on the *Glacier* or stuck on Stellamira. You've got that much choice, and only that much, and I'm not even going to ask you which you choose. So come on, and I'll show you what we're doing about the holds to hold the people that we're going to take off that devil-ridden planet tonight."

He walked to the back of the engine room,

through another bulkhead, into another child's toy of a tunnel, and pushed through another bulkhead at its side. That bulkhead opened into a sort of spiral slide that led down to an ice floor much farther down than I had expected to find in this ship, and stretching a good kilometer from forward to back. It was a hold, circled around the central corridor, and the floor of the hold was about forty meters down.

It wasn't so much the size of the hold, but the way it was rigged that got to me. There were ropes. Not just a few ropes, but grids and nets of ropes. Gallagher swung out along them confidently.

"Can't have people just sitting on the ice in here," he said, "and I didn't have enough material for proper decking. So—well, I reckon this is about as good a crash deck as anybody could rig."

The plane of interwoven "decking" that we were traversing was at an angle of about 45° to the current direction of gravity—that is, gravity due to spin. Suddenly Gallagher sat down and allowed himself to protrude somewhat through the fairly wide mesh.

"They can lie down like this and not be particularly uncomfortable whether we're on spin gravity or drive gravity. It's almost as good as a hammock."

I'd been carefully matching Gallagher as we made our way across this thing, trying to keep my mind from actually confronting what he'd told me about the *Starfire*. Now I tried the webbing. It looked comfortable, but in actual practice it wasn't. I stretched out, and the ropes were soft, but there weren't enough of them. I could prop my feet and not slide, or I could even let my feet dangle through. But I couldn't get the idea that it would be anything but an awkward way to travel.

"Don't think I'd be highly comfortable here," I said, and Gallagher swung back up into position for leaving.

"Doesn't make the best accommodations you could think of, does it? But really, the company didn't leave us much choice. We managed to liberate this rope from one of their warehouses. It's actually cable they use for mining. Soft and plastic, but tough. And extremely strong. Anybody who can manage to bring himself along a hammock or something of the sort will be ahead of the game, and lord knows those people have already had enough problems without facing them with a mode of transportation like this. But it was the best we could do with the materials at hand."

Beyond the ropes there were men working around the floor of the hold, and there was a glare from infrared heaters strung in a seemingly haphazard manner around the floor. A blast of heat rose from that surface that I certainly wouldn't expect to be compatible with ice. I assumed the melt was running off in channels and being pumped to the outside.

Gallagher stood there on the ropes surveying the scene. "We've got it pretty near big enough already," he said with some satisfaction. Then he turned and started back to the bulkhead. I followed.

But now I could no longer keep my mind blanked. The *Starfire* was gone. My commission —I was a space nut, theoretically, if not in the bleak actuality that had almost happened. But I was *not* a space nut. I *was* captain of the *Starfire*. And I would have to find a way to get to Earth to reestablish myself properly. . . .

We reached the bridge, and Gallagher flung himself into the captain's seat, but I remained standing.

"You're taking the people off Stellamira— evacuating it?" I asked, rather forlornly I'm afraid.

"What would you do—abandon them to the company finks who are out for blood now you've been rescued?" Gallagher's voice was hard.

I shook my head. You couldn't do that, I realized. "Even so, it's piracy," I said. "Or something like that."

"It's a rescue mission," he said shortly. "That planet's murder, the way it's being run."

"The way it's being run could be changed," I said weakly. Then: "It clouds the issue, just hauling them off like this," I added stubbornly. "The company would have the right to send armed ships after them."

I paused, and then in spite of my better sense, I went on. "The colonists have rights. The right to leave. Fair enough. But they *do* owe a debt to the company, and if they just up and leave without paying the debt; then the Space Commission has to go after them, or the company can take military measures of redress. And there are other planets in the same fix, or at least nearly so. So if you cloud the issue, legally, that is . . ."

Gallagher looked at me curiously. "You're right," he said, "in a sort of half-assed legal way. There's some might even hesitate because of that fact. But they're being treated like animals, and that no man can tolerate."

"They could acknowledge the debt," I said desperately.

He thought about that for a minute, then his face broke into a huge grin. "Sign an IOU? By God, Harald, that they could. And on the planet I've in mind for them, they can set up and repay the debt before any Space Commission that ever existed could even get through the first investigation—much less issue permits for armed intervention. With me to handle their shipping and their marketing for them, they could," he added modestly.

Gallagher generously offered to let me stay aboard the *Glacier* during the evacuation proceedings—war would be a better term for it. "No use you and your ideals getting mixed up in a pirate operation," he said soothingly.

I refused the privilege point-blank. "It's a legal operation, handled, I'll admit, somewhat illegally; but there will only be violence if the colonists' right to leave is obstructed," I said. "I would be proud to be part of it, and will be able to report the details more exactly, as an eyewitness, when I appear before the Space Commission as soon as I can find transport to Earth."

"Your faith in the Space Commission is touching," he answered sarcastically, but he made me second in command aboard the *Glacier* and gave

me the coordinates of the planet he had in mind
for the Stellamirans before we went down.

"Just in case a Gallagher's luck turns black,"
he said.

FOUR

There are no guns on a planet where the populace is as thoroughly controlled as it was Stellamira, except those in the hands of the company police; and since officials tend to think of weapons in terms of guns, the populace was considered unarmed.

A preconceived notion like that will do more to keep Authority (upper-case) comfortable and unsuspicious than any other factor, and Suzie had seen to it that that complacent attitude was not disabused.

Yet a man with a laser gun is absolutely helpless when he's writhing under a jolt of 10,000 to 20,000 volts of electricity being applied by a contraption that is essentially a battery-powered water pistol.

No one in authority noticed or cared when the colonists started making their kids water pistols with two tiny jets spaced four to eight centimeters apart. The tiny atomic batteries they have these days are so useful for powering things like flashlights that Authority didn't bother about them either. Yet those tiny batteries are equally useful for powering high-energy circuits if the circuit is pulsed; and given a high-energy pulse applied to a dual stream of mildly salted water—well, you've got a fairly efficient little electrocution circuit. The power isn't enough to kill, but it sure can make a man dance while you knock the laze pistol out of his hand with a stick or other nonconductive agent.

Then there was a ghastly weapon, borrowed from way back in history—a combination of palmitic acid and naphtha, originally called napalm, I believe, though when I went to look it up later I found it classified as Greek fire and a good many other terms for incendiary chemicals that have been used in wars as far back as the ancient records go. It hadn't been particularly difficult for the colonists to get hold of the materials for that one, either. For palmitic acid they substituted common soap; and for the naphtha, any light hydrocarbon oil that burns freely. There were plenty of those around, the fuels commonly used in ground cars—oils and gasolines.

They had come up with a sticky brown jelly which, if you got it on you was very difficult to get off and would burn where it stuck. Lethal. A small paper bag of the stuff thrown at almost anything——personnel or building—would stick and burn a hot, deadly flare, for three or four minutes.

Then there were rocks. Stellamira is practically made of rocks. Man, woman, boy, and girl, the Stellamiran colonists had formed the habit of "taking out their frustrations" by throwing rocks. That's why they said they were doing it, and that's how it looked. Practicing was the real reason. Target practice. They threw rocks on the way to and from the mines. They threw rocks in any free time they might have. They made games centered around throwing rocks in the bits and pieces of time they had free. The games had names and were competitive, and the colonists became accurate with rocks.

Why the constant guards didn't tumble to that one I don't know. If the kids had had balls to play games with and had shown a preference for rocks, it might have aroused attention. But kids and something to throw are normal; and if the grownups join in the game, why the paternalistic attitude is that it's a good way to take out their normal grumble-pattern.

Slingshots were kept less in evidence, but they weren't hidden and they were practiced. And a throwing sling that the colonists invented—actually, it went back to the days of David and Goliath—was simply a leather cup with three strings. You put a rock in the pouched leather, take two ends of strings on two fingers, and hang on to the third with your thumb while you whirl the thing; then let go with your thumb and throw. Makes a good sap, too, at close quarters; but at long distance it can be accurate (with practice) up to twenty meters or so.

That executive complacency, the assumption by the corporate finks and the guards that they were dealing with unarmed colonists, had been a major factor in the planning of the revolution. The intercolonist discipline that kept the newly developing abilities from being used in any quarrels had been a no-questions-asked extermination.

The revolution started while we were on our

way down—timed to the instant when we would be just outside detection range but well on our way to the port. The internal timing had been planned in detail. It was only the date that had changed.

The first and last parts of the revolution were organized in a manner that would have put even Clausewitz to shame for strategy and purpose. The center part got a bit disorganized, but that's expectable. You turn that many people loose who have been treated like cattle for long enough to make them furious but not long enough to make them over into cattle, you're going to get mayhem. You got mayhem. Berserk is a term that comes to mind.

The company armory and communications systems were the first targets. The riot-control equipment was in the armory, and the guards and their corporation execs depended on communications—from telephone to walkie-talkie. The colonists didn't depend on communications. With the kind of furious purpose you had there, all you had to have was advance planning so everybody knew the general outline. After that, runners were sufficient.

Suzie gave an impromptu party that night, and since the thing had been planned for a year, she'd made a habit of impromptu parties. They were accepted as normal. This was at the glittery part of Suzie's, the "Company and Off-Planet Personnel Only" part. It was mostly for off-duty guards, though a number of executives always made excuses to come.

At the height of the party, as had become a

custom, some of Suzie's girls were dispatched to take refreshments and the pleasure of their company to the guards at the armory and the police station.

It was timed. The dope went into all the drinks at the same time. Where a guard didn't drink fast enough, there were a sufficiency of the little roller's taps around to finish the job, and the girls were alert and watching to see which was needed where—and fast.

There were a few of the guards—even one or two of the executives—that the girls had decided were "franks" instead of "finks," and for this Suzie was prepared, too. A big lipsticked "F" went on each forehead. The official franks weren't trusted too far, though. They were marked and locked in a small room at Suzie's until takeoff time.

Almost as the guards went down to the dope and the taps, the girls inside opened the barred doors, and the task forces of colonists assigned to those jobs moved into the armory and the police station.

At the same moment, a group of colonists was frantically digging down to a main communications and power cable. The power cable was left for last. That would alert the corporate headquarters. It was the communications cable that they tackled, and the two best technicians among the colonists had been assigned that job, surrounded by an armed mob for possibly needed protection.

They didn't cut the cable. That would have presented the finks with a simple problem, open and shut, recognizable for what it was. Instead, they set up a random pulser that caused the automatic equipment associated with the land-wires to go berserk. Phone systems have switching facilities for only 15 to 20 percent of their lines at a time. The random pulser kept initiating a few hundred simultaneous calls, and it not only put the communications lines out of order quite effectively, it tied corporate brains up at a critical point.

Then too, a self-powered, random-pulse sweep generator—probably the most complicated installation it had been felt necessary to build secretly prior to the revolution—was turned on. Walkie-talkies, planetary and off-planet communications were instantly jammed, except for a single narrow-band notch in the spectrum that would allow the port-control facility to stay in contact with Gallagher's *Glacier* and the landing tugs as soon as the port was captured.

It was then that the power cables were cut. That signaled to the corporation as nothing else could that this one was for real.

The war was on. But the armory and the police station were already in the hands of the colonists, and a good many of the guards were out of action.

But this was still the critical point of the revolution, and it was here that the real genius of Gallagher and Suzie showed—the genius that knows its opponent and uses his strength as a weakness. The judo-genius—or perhaps karate would be the better term.

There would be two major points that the corporation would, by its nature, defend first and with the greatest ferocity. Of these the first would be the "treasure house"—the warehouses where the starstones and rare earths waited for shipment. The second would be the port itself, where twenty freighter tugs waited to load incoming ships.

The port we had to have; but the "treasure house" was so much dross to the colonists, and Gallagher and Suzie had made sure they knew it. They couldn't have marketed the starstones if they'd gotten them—not without greater hazard than they were worth. The corporate execs should have known that, but in the planning, Gallagher and Suzie gambled that the instinct to protect the treasure would be stronger than any logical reasoning they might have time to indulge.

So the attack on company headquarters was two-pronged instead of three-pronged. The colonists came in through the entrances to the port and to the colonists' area, but they left the way to the warehouses open. And, like sheep, the corporates ran to the treasure house. It was beautiful. They followed the instinct to protect the treasure and they followed the path of least resistance. The two were the same.

Then the colonists could simply keep up a sniper fire around the warehouses and leave the finks where they were—holed up guarding what was essentially valueless in terms of winning or losing the war. Effectively out of the action. Effectively prisoners guarded by only a medium-sized group.

That was probably the bit of know-how that actually won the revolution, though the war was far from ending as we set down, not much later, and joined the melee.

Oh, it wasn't over when we set down. Not by a long shot. There was fighting everywhere.

There was one odd advantage the colonists had. That was the short focal range of the corporate lasers. To be effective, a laser has to be focused, and it's a delicate job requiring at least half an hour. They're prefocused. The people who had armed the guards had considered a short focal range to be optimum. It prevented accidental destruction of company property under riot conditions. That was one place the notion that the populace was unarmed showed its results. The guards were effectively limited to the same range as the colonists. A slingshot can be accurate to probably no more than twenty meters, a water pistol at six to eight.

A ground skimmer gave the advantage of range, since you could come at your target at sixty kilometers an hour; but the skimmers were in the hands of both sides by the time things were well underway.

We set down, and the others scattered to their assigned tasks, whatever they may have been. Gallagher had given me orders to stay on the port; to see to it that the freighter tugs were operational; and to supervise the actual evacuation. A sort of blanket kind of orders. The port was swarming with colonists, and though I had a big red lipstick F on my forehead, I had little else to tell them I was on their side. I wasn't in uniform, which may have helped.

I headed for the nearest tug. Nobody opposed me until I reached it and was opening the hatch, when about sixteen cobbers all had their hands on me at once. There was scatterlight, but that's an eerie kind of light, and it felt like a million people grabbing me. Lurid imagination. Sixteen's a good guess.

"Gallagher gave me orders!" I shouted.

The hands became gentler, and I was set on my feet, actually unharmed as yet. Instantly I went into captain's gear.

"Can any of you men handle a tug?" I asked in my best voice-of-authority. "We've got to get these tugs operational."

A big fellow next to me, examining the *F* on my forehead, grunted. "Don't know you, Cobber," he said grimly.

"I'm Dundee, formerly of the *Starfire*. I came down from the *Glacier* with Gallagher."

The big man gestured to an only slightly smaller one nearby. "Get in the tug with him, Brant. If he does anything wrong, kill him."

That was all. I climbed in the hatch, Brant right behind me, but before he slammed the hatch shut I saw a company car shoot onto the field, gunning people down and heading straight our way.

I jumped to the pilot's couch and switched on the warmup, calling to Brant at the same time. "Strap down. We'll get the atomic motors bearing on that skimmer."

There wasn't time, but it didn't matter. Brant seemed to trust that answer, for he strapped in.

As the screens lit, they showed one of the strangest sights I've ever seen. Instead of running away, the big man and his gang were running *toward* that vehicle—a wave of men, women and even some small enough to be children, that grew as it surged toward the skimmer for others on the field answered his shouted instructions and joined.

There were bright flashes of laze guns from the three or four guards in the car, but then the skimmer was onto the wave of people, and every one within reach grabbed at its tail and flipped.

The thing flipped over, its momentum barely slowed, and skated along on its top, losing speed rapidly. The people ran to catch up. As they reached it, they jumped onto it, and the next clear view I got that skimmer looked like a tin can that had been stomped flat. There were parts of guards sticking out all over it.

By then the tug motors were warmed, and I got it up on its ground effect. Brant was standing over me at that point, not sure what I was going to do, but I eased the tug carefully past the crowd and back to the one port entrance where that skimmer had come in and where others might follow it. Then I set the tug down with its tail facing into the entrance. As the next car burst through, I was ready and waiting for it, with the tug sitting firmly, ground effect off. Under that condition, I could feed about half power into the forward thrust jets without moving the vehicle. As that second skimmer came into line with the jet, it was picked up as though by a giant hand and rose a good forty meters into the air, flipping as it went. Nobody had to stomp that one after it came down.

I looked around then, and Brant was grinning all over his face. He was a heavy man, with a heavy-lined face; and every line creased with dirt; but he looked alive and the grin was as fierce as it was happy.

"Think you could handle this post?" I asked him, putting all the authority I knew how to put into the question.

"You show me how just once more, I'll handle it," he said happily.

I must have taken ten minutes checking him out. I wasn't sure when I left that he was clear on why what worked that I showed him how to work, but I'd made him go over the sequence until I was sure he had it pat. If determination could do the job, he'd do it. So I climbed out and began looking for the big man who'd first accosted me. He seemed to be in charge, more or less.

In that soft light, with the number of people around, you'd think I'd have trouble finding one man. I didn't. I wandered until I found a youngster who was looking as though for what his next job might be. "Where's the big man in charge?" I asked.

"Bill?"

I nodded and he seemed satisfied. "This way," he said and took me straight to the man. Seems I'd lucked into one of the runners.

I walked straight up to Bill. "I need pilots for these tugs," I said, as though I were in command, not he.

"Nice job with the tug," he commented, then turned to the youngster, gave him a list of names I didn't bother listening to.

"Have them meet me there," I said, pointing out a tug. Then I turned to leave.

The big man's hand clamped down on my arm, and I turned back, ready for trouble. But it wasn't trouble.

"I don't know how good any of them are as pilots," he growled down at me. "If you've got a way of checking them out, check them out. They're the best we've got, but we haven't had tugs to practice on much, you know."

I nodded. Then I added lightly, "We don't really have a space academy here to choose from, do we?"

Instantly his face went hard. "Don't underrate 'em, mister," he said fiercely, and I thought for a moment that hand on my shoulder was going to shake me like a rat. "A slummer can't get into the academies. All he can get into is a colonist's berth. But that don't mean he can't handle a skimmer and translate on out from that, with enough drive behind him. I'm sending you the guys that had the drive."

"I'm not underrating," I said as grimly as he. "But I'm not planning to mess up the tugs before we get the *Glacier* loaded, either."

He nodded, as though I'd satisfied whatever was eating him, and let go my shoulder. I don't think it was a shove he gave me as he let go; just that his hand so powerful that it shoved when it was being gentle.

The guys that reported, as fast as they got the

message and could get to me, were actually beyond my best expectations. Two of them I'd already seen on the *Glacier* and on the lander coming down. In spite of what Bill had said, they'd all of them actually handled tugs one time or another, when the corporation had needed more than the one or two pilots it kept on hand. I checked each one out, and I kept most of them, for I needed twenty and I didn't have many more than that. I proved wrong about only one, but I didn't find that out until he got one group of passengers safely aboard the *Glacier* and was landing for his next set. He may really have known what he was doing. It may have been a malfunction, or just barely possibly somebody up in the ivory tower had managed to rerange one of the short-range lasers and had done some damage as he came in. I saw the machine stagger while it was still two hundred meters in the air, and then veer off course.

I speculated later that it must have been either sheer luck or real guts on the part of that pilot, but I guess I'll never know. The tug staggered and veered off course. Then it dropped a little and gained speed. It must have been doing right at a thousand kilometers an hour. It was probably as much the sonic wave in front of it as it was the actual mass of the ship that simply blew the tower apart.

I understand the colonists officially decided later that the pilot was a hero and had done it on purpose. I've never really been able to make up my mind. He could have been dead of a laser shot before the sequence of action took place, though if that ship wasn't guided by the pilot on board, it was very definitely hurled by the hatred of the crowd that was watching.

By then the revolution itself was pretty much a mopping-up operation, and my part in it had settled into a routine of getting passengers and all the luggage they could carry into tugs and off for the *Glacier*. I decided to leave the tug guarding the gate where it was, just in case. That left us with eighteen freighters plus Gallagher's lander, and we kept them moving. It was probably more to the credit of the people who had taken over the traffic control system of the port than it was to my own efforts that we were able to keep the tugs moving, one after the other, at a slow but steady pace. I don't yet know whether it was days or hours later when we began loading the tugs more and more with liberated equipment and less and less with people.

Somewhere along about there I began to get foggy and was shoved aside to a corner to sleep for a while. When I woke the job was still going on, and I started doggedly back to it.

One of Suzie's girls barred my way. "Not yet, captain," she said. "You go over there and go through that chow line first."

In astonishment I saw that tables and fires had been rigged. Food was being served. Hot and nourishing, with hot, nourishing drinks. Suzie's girls. Efficient and even cheerful. There were deep circles under their eyes, as well as numbers of bandages on their bodies. One girl was on a crutch improvised out of a board and some rags stuffed under her arm for padding.

She was working right along with the rest.

The deep circles and pale faces contrasted to heavy lipstick and makeup that I gather they'd not had time to remove. I realized then that Suzie's girls would have been the ones best organized on the planet. The ones handling the mechanical details such as food and record keeping. Sure enough, near enough the food area to be part of the efficiency there was a group on old boxes with notebooks and paper, keeping the best track they could of what had gone and what was yet to go, checking against lists.

What kind of girl could do a job like that after a life like that, I wondered briefly; but I took my hat off to them mentally and returned their smiles and cheerfulness to the best of my still-groggy ability.

There were few refugees left on the field, and they were trickling one or two at a time into the continuously loading tugs. But now the tugs were taking mostly heavy equipment, ton after ton. Mining equipment. Air-powered drills. Self-propelled atomic-power supplies. Bulldozers and graders. All the things that go to make up both deep-mining and strip-mining equipment, to say nothing of ton after ton of ropes and explosives and less-complicated machinery that would be useful in setting up a planet.

Eventually I turned to check what was to be loaded on the next ship, and found there wasn't a full load left to go. I got the loading started, then put in a call to Port Control. I told them that no more than two of the tugs aloft were to be allowed to come back. The rest were now ordered to secure themselves onto the *Glacier* after they unloaded. We weren't going to strip the port completely. One of the two tugs I allowed to return was to remain here, as well as the one still sitting at the gate.

Aboard the last tug we loaded the remaining personnel—the control-room men, the loaders themselves, and three of Suzie's girls who hadn't gone up yet. Gallagher had gone up some time since. I looked around for Suzie.

She and Seth were at a distance, working over something on the ground. It looked like a radio antenna of some sort. I called to them. Suzie waved absently, intently standing over Seth, who was pushing down on something that seemed not to give. Then it gave, and at the same moment my attention was distracted by a number of explosions in the port area.

I ran toward Suzie and Seth, who were gathering up whatever piece of equipment they'd been working on.

"The war's started up again," I shouted even before I was near enough. "We're too few down here now. Come on."

Seth already had the equipment in his arms, and was trailing Suzie as she turned to go past me, walking fast and hard. I turned with her, and she looked up at me.

"That wasn't more war," she said. Her eyes were steel-bright. "That was us. We've just destroyed the evidence of how this 'spontaneous uprising' was engineered."

That startled me, but I didn't have much time to think. Suzie and Seth ducked into the hatch of that final tug, and I was turning to climb in when I realized, more by instinct than anything else, that there was one person left behind.

I turned to wave at the tug sitting next to the skimmer gate and saw through the gate, a group of about twenty skimmers come roaring down the lane toward the port. Apparently some of the company finks had realized that nearly everyone was gone, and that as we were evacuating the last of the people, we would be vulnerable. They were out to make the most of it.

There was nothing I could do but watch and hold my breath. Then, as the first of the skimmers came opposite the tug, it went hurtling into the air from the blast of the thruster, and I found myself breathing again, though the air I breathed held the acrid sting of smoke. The paint of the tug behind me was scorching, and I realized that the corporates had had time to refocus their lasers.

One after another, six of the skimmers, going too fast to stop, were hurled into the air. One after another they landed in a heap. The other skimmers managed to stop before they reached the catastrophe point.

The tug I was beside began maneuvering to put its blast toward the gate. Not on it, for that would have isolated our defending tug. Just near enough. The rest of the skimmers saw it and were backing away, fast. The hatch of the tug by the gate flung open. A figure emerged from it and started to run toward me.

Brant was almost beside me before I turned to climb into our tug . . . and stumbled over, just

behind where I had been standing, the scorched
and crumpled body of one of Suzie's girls.

I stood and stared. The laze must have missed
me by micrometers. I almost wished it hadn't.
She looked so pathetic—a small doll thrown into
the fire and lying, half consumed, beside the
ashes.

Then Brant was pushing me from behind. I
stumbled on into the tug, sick with rage but
knowing that the job was to get this last ship up.

The trip to the planet that the colonists decided to call Refuge was rough, but uneventful.
Yet it had one detour that came as a complete
surprise to me.

It was rough for the refugees, but there was
nothing we could do about that. They seemed to
think the discomfort a small price to pay, for as
far as I ever heard there was not a single com-
plaint. The leadership that they organized—
they were actually fairly well organized before
that last tug got up—kept the complaints to
themselves, if there were any.

At Gallagher's suggestion, we left them alone.
"They've got to handle their own problems," he
told me. "Best they start right now." We went
down together, about once daily, on inspection
tours, but that was all.

Suzie's girls had a smallish compartment forward of the big holds and aft of the bridge. I had
wondered what the relationship between the
girls and the other women would be when they
were all together in that hold, and was rather
relieved at the separation. I gathered, too, that

the girls' compartment was "closed to business" which seemed quite sensible on shipboard. Some relationships have to work themselves out in more spacious areas. The girls had been the major heroes of the revolution. The women among the colonists couldn't exclude them. But, considering the jealousies that would inevitably be involved, I couldn't see their being accepted either.

I had a lot to learn.

Suzie herself shared Gallagher's cabin, and Seth bunked in with me. Seth was Suzie's right-hand man and her devoted slave. It was a strange relationship: more that of a dog to his mistress than anything else, and I'm quite sure it wasn't anything else. He was the brawn for her brain, and quite content with the role. I think it fulfilled him far more than any other relationship with any other human could have done.

I didn't even begin to understand Suzie and her forty girls until that first hour in the control cabin. Even that was just a beginning. I guess I never will understand completely, but I can admire and respect.

Gallagher was setting up our course; Suzie was in the co-pilot's couch. I was in what might have been termed the navigator's couch, a couch with just a place for writing, no controls. Seth was in the tiny galley fixing coffee. We were all bushed, but far too stimulated and exuberant to relax.

Suzie was lighting a cigarette as she said quietly to Gallagher, "Set your course for Durango."

He looked at her in surprise. "Thought we'd

get the colonists to their planet, then you and the girls would take some time off at Betsy Ann with me," he said. "It's time for a vacation."

Suzie shook her head, just gently, but there was no question in her voice. "Durango," she said. "We're going to escape from you. You forced us to go along when you evacuated Stellamira, so there'd be no witnesses. But we found some guns and stuff and hijacked your *Glacier* and made you drop us there."

He nodded slowly. "It's a good story," he said, "and you'll be welcomed because the local talent isn't much and it isn't many, and it isn't set up like you set up. I worked on Durango as an electrical engineer for several months awhile back. But why bother? We can whomp up a good story when you're ready. Anyhow," he added savagely, "one revolution ought to be enough for any one or all of you."

She smiled. Then: "That one was for my husband. The next one will be for my baby. And then there are all the other kids we might have had. The company killed them as surely as they did Jack and the baby. Not even fast. Slow. The rest of the girls feel the same way. It's not a single corporation we're after, it's the system. It's the system that killed our men and our way of life. It's the system that's got to go."

She went on, and her voice had a dreamy quality to it. "It's not even that the system has to go. It's the system we're going to kill. Us. With our bare hands if we could. With our bare asses since we can't. We're murderers and we're pragmatists. But the murderer part comes first.

With each and every one of us. Killers. Deadly. And deadly with purpose."

I was staring at her, dumbfounded, as she leaned back relaxed, smoking. She was slender and quite beautiful in her intent way.

"Dublin," she said quietly, "you're just a revolutionist. You're a revolutionist because you don't like the system and because revolution is more fun than any other game. You're not a killer, but one revolution won't satisfy you, any more than killing one company—and the Stellamira Company is dead." She chuckled. "Its assets are disbursed. It won't be able to come back, though another company will take over. Until we kill the system, other companies will take over.

"Killing the system will satisfy you. You're just a revolutionist. One revolution will only whet your appetite. It's addictive. Two will addict you more. You won't be satisfied even with ten or twenty or thirty. But you'll be satisfied when the system's licked.

"That's the difference. You'll be satisfied and turn to something else. We—all of us—will be finished when that happens. What do you do after you're finished is something I haven't started to think about yet. Maybe I'll come to Betsy Ann then. It's a long *then*. Don't wait for me."

"Oh, I won't wait," Gallagher answered lightly. "Maybe I'll even let you finish this one off before I kidnap you and make you fight 'em my way."

"Hell," Suzie said. "Your way's fine, but it's not nearly as efficient. You're envious because you aren't equipped to be as efficient at the revolution business as we are. The idea of women running the show still shocks you a bit. You might even be a bit jealous. Not of our so-called profession, but of our position which gives us the possibility of handling revolutions more successfully than you can." She started to laugh, and then Gallagher started to laugh.

Then Seth's voice came from the galley, slow, like it was finding each word in turn, and each one required hunting for.

"Gallagher could get into your revolutions the way I have," he said. There was laughter under his slow voice. "There's always room for a man in a house."

At that they began to laugh aloud, deep, satisfying belly laughs, and I was the one who was jealous, looking from one to the other, unbelieving. It wasn't funny. It was bloody and horrible and sad and pathetic and we'd just left a real bloodbath in which real people—colonists and company alike—had been killed. And it was murder Suzie was avenging. It wasn't funny.

But underneath I could hear Gallagher's voice from way back: *It takes a free man to laugh, and it takes laughter to set a man free.* Perhaps that was it? But they weren't free! They were bound to a life harder than any I had dreamed of. To a life of revolution and murder. It wasn't funny.

Then I put my oar in. "I guess I'd better go down to Durango with you," I said. "I could have been kidnapped in the same way you were, and helped with the hijacking. Then I could get a ship back to Earth and report to the Space Commission. . . ."

I trailed off, for the laughter had stopped and they were all looking at me kindly, like parents interrupted in a grown-up discussion by a childish question.

"Harald," Suzie said gently, "you'd be clapped in prison the instant you set foot on Durango. They'd signal your company, and the company would signal back, and you'd be in irons. You haven't the—talents—we have to make you welcome any other way."

"But how am I going to get to Earth and report so that this whole situation changes?" I asked. "That's the real job that's got to be done."

Suzie opened her mouth, then closed it again. Seth started to speak, but while he was organizing his words, Gallagher interrupted.

"Time enough," he said with a finality in his tone that ended the discussion. "Time enough, when we get to it."

FIVE

We dropped Suzie and her gang at Durango and the colonists at Refuge. Then we drove for Beta Antolaris.

They call it Betsy Ann, both the planet and the system. It's the second system that was explored by Dr. Antolar's original survey, back when the Antolaric drive was first invented. Betsy Ann is the planet that Gallagher colonized from the house he bought out, and with the wolves that he selected.

Beta Antolaris is a nine-planet system, comparable in most respects to the Sol system itself, including a large ring of asteroids in the fifth orbit. It surprised me that Gallagher didn't go directly in to the third planet on approaching the system, but instead put us into orbit around one of the outer ice giants and radioed for a taxi.

"But why orbit so far out?" I asked. "And why not use your own landing craft?"

Gallagher frowned at me. "Since when have you tried any interplanetary jumps with a landing tug? They're not designed to do anything but very minor maneuvers in space, since, as you darned well know, they use atmosphere for most of the thrust they build up. You could get to

Betsy Ann Three from here with a landing tug if you didn't mind taking months doing it. But at that you'd probably be all out of maneuvering mass and have to send an SOS down to the planet before you could land. Anyhow, the taxis are running fairly regular and it won't take one much out of its way to come past and fetch us.

"As for orbiting out here," he went on quickly before I could interrupt, "why, the *Glacier* wouldn't have a life expectancy of two years, if I orbited her regular around a standard planet." The phrase startled me, coming from Gallagher in spite of the fact that it's the usual term for a planet in all respects similar to Earth.

"It would melt?"

Gallagher shook his head. "Evaporate," he said. "I sort of think we may be on Betsy Ann awhile, and it's better to leave Baby here in the deep freeze."

I did a quick calculation in my head. If the system were anywhere near an approximation of the Sol system, we'd be twenty-nine to thirty times farther out from the local sun than the third planet; and by the inverse-square law, would get something like one over 850-to-1 over 900 the amount of radiation in the form of light.

I nodded. "So you can extend a parking orbit quite a long time out here," I said, "and not be using even standby power."

"Add a bit of mass while we're about it. Increase rather than decrease our size," he said. "Not by much, but appreciable."

I was surprised and must have shown it, for Gallagher answered my unspoken question. He leaned forward and his voice took on the intent tone it only held when he was challenged by a problem. You might say that he slipped into engineering gear, much the way I slip into captain's gear.

"Anytime you'd care to check it out," he said, "I think you'll find that the planetary orbits correspond fairly well with the charged particle crossover points dues to the magnetic and electrostatic fields in the system of any sun. Any sun —or any rotating planet, for that matter—has magnetic and electrostatic fields that trap particles. Like the orbiting electron and proton belts of Earth," he added impatiently when he saw that I didn't understand.

"The magnetic and electrostatic fields of a sun, acting on the solar wind of charged particles thrown off by that sun, create, in effect, a mass spectrograph—with the particles fanned out by charge and weight into separate spiral orbits of each individual type of particle.

"This mass spectrograph has focal points at or close to logarithmic centers which are the crossover points of the spirals of the various types of individuated particles. These focal points will be the places where the particles of various charges and weights tend to come together in one orbit, neutralize each other, and then simply continue to build up until they form a mass which will eventually accrete to the size of a planet. So the planets are actually focal points in the mass spectrograph that the sun creates by its existence.

"Since the planets are found," he repeated

himself, "at the points of intersection where the acceleration orbits of charged particles overlap, we can know that the ice giants like the one out there have very good focal-point relationships for accreting—guess what?"

"Hydrogen and oxygen, of course, if the solar wind is fanned out as a mass spectrograph; and I rather imagine you're right," I said.

"Check it out," he suggested. "It checks. And yes, this is a crossover point on the hydrogen and oxygen spirals, so they predominate. Even so, accretion by the ship wouldn't be very great— the first steps in planetary formation are slow— if we simply placed the *Glacier* in this orbit alone. You need the mass of that planet for any appreciable effect. At that, accretion is hardly likely to exceed evaporation by more than a few percent."

I was fascinated, and I sat there picturing the effect. Seeing the vast magnetic and electrostatic fields created by the sun forming overlapping patterns around their fiery source. Where they overlapped, their interactions formed giant lenses, and through those lenses poured the twisting tornado of the solar wind, its torrent of motion reaching the lenses as a sunbeam reaches a prism. I watched that wind of ionized particles fan out through the lenses into its component parts, like a light ray bent through a prism; but while a light ray bent through a prism separates into its differing frequencies fanned into separate but straight pathways that show as differing colors, this mass spectrograph fanned its particles into spiral patterns that must eventually cross and recross in a complex series of focal points that would orbit their sun, held by the very forces that had created them, and would spin more and more closely together as they accreted into planets. . . .

While I sat thinking, Gallagher was inching us into orbit, correcting and recorrecting in an attempt to perfect our swing around that huge ice world. Then, just as he was making a final maneuver, there was a voice on the radio—a woman's voice—and at the same time a flaring red light on the control panel.

Gallagher reached over and switched on the radio transmitter. His voice crackled out: "Damn it, steer that taxi away until I get this berg properly in orbit. You're overloading my detectors."

"Sorry, honey." The voice that came back was a rich contralto, and not nearly as formal as one might expect. "But has it occurred to you that you might be overloading my detectors, too? I was doing a scientific—"

"Scientific be damned! I'm glad you're here, anyhow. You can give us a lift back to Betsy Three."

"Okay, Gallagher."

Gallagher hadn't said he was Gallagher, and how the devil the pilot of that other ship knew who she was talking to I hadn't a clue. Of course, Gallagher was the only guy in space so far as anybody knew that was running around in an iceberg for a ship, but it hardly seemed to me that anybody on a security watch would simply take it for granted that this was Gallagher's ship.

What one man has done, another man can do; and it was more than possible that one of the corporations would set up an iceberg just to fool somebody. I said as much, but Gallagher only laughed.

"You're perfectly right, Harald, if that were the end and the all of it. But I assure you that we've got just as good IFFs on our ships as any that the corporations have on theirs."

I felt properly deflated. Of course, no traffic pattern would be set up without proper "Identification, Friend or Foe" transponders, if only because they make the operation of computer controllers much simpler.

To hide my discomfort, I began fiddling with the dials on the telescreen that showed a picture of nearby space, and almost at once I managed to overlap the red blinking dot with an actual picture of the taxi. Suddenly I strained forward. "Hey, that's not a taxi. That's—"

"A nickel-steel meteor," Gallagher finished for me dryly. "Though you can't properly call it a meteor until it actually touches atmosphere."

I held onto my voice for a moment, but then it came out in spite of me. "Crude construction," I said, though not haughtily. I'd learned at least that much. "I gather you use a great variety of space debris for transportation."

"Nothing like using what's handy," he answered laconically. "Though it won't be a ship long."

He pushed the button for a final micro-maneuver, then checked the orbit. Satisfied, he turned back to the radio and lit the screen.

It lighted to show a freckle-faced girl, hair

drawn back in a pony tail, and probably not over sixteen. Well, the pony tail and freckles could throw you off. The rest of the figure, under a tight pair of coveralls, gave her about twenty years, possibly a few more. Pretty responsible job for a youngster, and a girl at that, I thought; radio operator on a space vehicle, no matter how crude the construction.

"Okay, Cricket," Gallagher was saying. "You can taxi on in now."

"You forgot to turn on your homing signal, Addlepate," she told him cheerfully. "Want I should home in on you as a derelict for practice? Or are you going to make it easy for me?"

"Didn't think you'd need a signal after that last contact," he said, switching it on. "However, you have it now. I'd hate to try your guesstimating too far."

The meteor-ship ranged in fast, and soon we were shoving out our airlock. A few *spuuuts* on our suit rockets put us up against a corridor cut in the meteor. Not far back, the corridor went through an airlock and became what might be called a chamber, since it had structured walls and a control console.

And there was that chit of a girl at the controls, and nobody else in sight.

She was a pretty thing, but so darned young. She gestured us to strap down on foam mats on the floor, since obviously this asteroid-cum-ship was not exactly equipped for much in the way of conveniences for passengers.

Gallagher took off his helmet, and I followed his lead.

"Good to see you back, Dublin," she said as he stretched flat on the foam mat, strapping down. I followed suit.

"This here's Harald Dundee," he said. "Former captain in the Solspace merchant fleet. He's stopping off for a spell on his way through to Earth to complain to the Space Commission about how one of the colonies was being run."

She nodded noncommitally in my direction, said "Hold on," and shifted us into a type of drive I wasn't expecting. I felt like somebody had just stepped on me with a twelve-foot shoe. The foam beneath me squeezed thin and dropped me into a pocket I couldn't have gotten out of if I'd wanted to.

It went on that way for the best part of twenty minutes, then slacked off to a more or less standard gee pressure. Then the girl locked the board, got out of her acceleration couch, and said, "How about some food?"

I was getting my breath back, and I took my time, looking about meanwhile. The whole structure, as far as I could tell, was a prefabricated unit that could accommodate three people in a pinch, but was designed for one-man operation. I realized that it was simply shoved into a hole that passed through the center of gravity of the asteroid.

"This thing isn't really designed as a ship, is it?" I asked as I joined them at the tiny galley end of the chamber.

"Well, now, that depends on how you look at it." Gallagher waved his hand around the compact compartment. "The power unit is well designed for the purpose. But the purpose, as you may have guessed, is to come out here and pick up chunks of nickel-steel that we need back on Betsy Three. It's not particularly difficult to bore a hole in just the right place in one of these asteroids and set the drive unit right into it. Then it becomes a rather slow and cumbersome ship. But take that same drive unit without the hull, and it's a damn fast piece of get-up-and-scat machinery."

The trip wasn't as brief as I had somehow expected it to be, since we were using one of the most basic drives that have ever been built: a simple rocket-power device, although it operated on nuclear energy. The rocket itself was an ionic affair which could consequently use very low mass at very high ejection velocities. Even with the mass of the asteroid wedged around it, this thing was capable of better than a six-gee thrust for maneuvering, and could run better than one gee on continuous acceleration. At that, it took us nearly two weeks in the cramped quarters to get from where we had been to where we were going. And though I'm sure we were all being very decent about it, in that length of time any three people can get on each other's nerves.

Gallagher and the girl knew each other so well that they didn't bother to use names. It took me two days to find out that Cricket's name was Mary Joinson. It took me only about twenty minutes longer to put my big foot in my mouth while trying to pay her a compliment. As I recall, I said something about how amazed I was that one so young could handle a ship so well.

"Pooh," she said, "anybody that can throw a rock can figure an orbit."

"But for such a young lady to be trusted with so much responsibility," I started.

"Wait a minute, sonny. Who's calling who young and incompetent? Seems to me the corporation you worked for must have been really sticking its neck out to let you be pushing one of their ships around."

"I didn't say a word about incompetent," I complained.

"Nor should you—a captain who's lost his own ship."

"I was merely trying to say—"

"—that you don't think girls belong in space. Right? Well, you're wrong. So far I've landed about twenty-eight of these chunks, and that's something of a record. Anyhow, what's the maximum cargo weight you ever carried?"

I saw what was coming, and I did a quick estimate of how big this chunk of nickel-steel really was in terms of mass.

"But then, even though this is more mass, the mass I was carrying went farther and was really a bit more than just a raw chunk of steel," I insisted.

"You didn't capture it, bore it, and . . . anyhow, what's more valuable to a growing economy than a raw chunk of steel already refined and all you've got to do is drop it. . . ."

"*Drop* it?" I had a picture of this chunk of steel we were riding dropping through a planetary atmosphere. It would burn, of course; but what got through would cause an explosion—a crater hundreds of meters deep.

"How do you land these things, anyhow?" I asked in horror.

"We fly them down, of course."

My estimate of the weight came up and hit me over the head at that point. It didn't matter how many gees this prepackaged drive was good for —you simply don't land fifty to a hundred million tons of steel all in one chunk.

The more I thought about it, the more I broke out in a cold sweat. A chunk of steel this size wouldn't have area enough compared to its mass to slow down appreciably in any atmosphere I'd ever heard of. Even if it came out of orbit at a considerably lower velocity than any I thought would be practicable, the damn thing would make an awful big dent wherever it hit.

"I think I'd rather get out and walk," I said.

"Well, okay. If you insist, we'll give you a parachute."

Somehow the landing operation got to be a standard joke, with Gallagher and Cricket on one side and me on the other. I kept advancing theories of how such a chunk could be landed, and they kept shooting holes in them. By the time we had reached the planet and Gallagher and I were told to lie down on the acceleration mats, I was in a real sweat.

I was convinced there was no way at all to land a chunk of steel like this, and that we were all on the verge of suicide. The fact that Cricket had landed this way, by her own statement, a number of times, helped intellectually, but it didn't do a damned thing for the autonomic sensors in my stomach that kept telling me I was having suicide committed on me by a girl-child who was riding the controls of a real-life space-ship, instead of the toy ones she should have been playing with.

First she got on the radio to party or parties unknown, presumably on the planet below. I told my stomach to shut up while I listened and watched the dials.

She didn't say much. Just alerted somebody that we were coming (smashing?) in.

She was too young to be at the controls. She was a girl. But she was in the captain's couch, and if you try to do anything about that, it's mutiny in any language. So why I watched the controls I don't know. I'd have been happier if I hadn't. Or hadn't listened to what she was saying over the radio. But I did, and I got un-happy and clenched my fists but I kept them at my sides.

Gallagher seemed relaxed.

As a method of easing my nervousness, I kept trying to stare at the unpainted wall of the tiny chamber, but my eyes kept straying back past Cricket's youthful figure toward the nav scope and the dials. There was nothing for my ears to hear but the susurrus of the ventilating fan and the ship's radio.

I had forced my attention back to the wall, seeking some imperfection to focus on, when I was brought back sharply by a raucous voice on the radio.

"Ground control to Taxi X-9. That's a good orbit, Cricket, but you're about nine kilometers too high."

"Okay, ground control. Dropping nine kilo."

I gasped and clenched my teeth as I felt a crunch of drive thrust that nearly put me through the floor, followed by the sensation of the ship swinging in free fall; then another crunch. The reassuring chatter of the radio penetrated my self-centered attention.

"That's good. Locked on. We've got you, Cricket. Cut drive." With each radio phrase, there was Cricket's calm reply.

I didn't understand those particular communications, but that didn't bother me. We were safely in orbit now, scarcely a hundred kilometers above the surface. I relaxed and waited for the order to unstrap . . .

. . . when things went wrong with the feel again, and my gaze jumped to the dials.

It was impossible. We had settled into orbit. But it was true.

"We're falling!" I gasped. "Falling like a rock!"

If the girl cut in the drive fast, I recognized, she could pull out. Possibly. But the rate-of-approach indicator was gaining momentum with every passing second.

Gallagher's voice penetrated my preoccupation, calm, unconcerned. "Relax, Dundee. We're being landed by a new system we use on this planet."

The girl was obviously going to do nothing. While I reassured myself that she and Gallagher were aboard, too, and surely not risking their necks in what appeared to me suicidal inactivity, my "captain's gear" mind was desperately turning over the calculations that it could derive from the dials I could see over the girl's shoulder.

Rate of approach to nearest object in space—the planet—ruinous. Confirmation from the nav scope where the planet was swelling as though we were diving at full power. Orbital velocity. Capability of the suit packs of those aboard, and whether a braking trajectory into a parking orbit were possible . . .

. . . but the answer was way over in the red. Even with ten times the pack power in those suits, the answer was too far in the red.

And ground control giving orders as though this were the normal approach of a landing craft; rather than a steel meteor rocketing toward the planet.

"Adjust barometric pressure to nine nine eight point three two millibars."

And Cricket's voice, as though she weren't minutes from death: "Barometric pressure set to cycle to nine nine eight point three two millibars."

Obviously there was something that I didn't understand. I clenched my teeth and tried to convince all my senses that respond efficiently to the readings of dials and the knowledges they have been trained to use. Those senses didn't convince worth a damn, but intellectually I guess I was convinced that the ship was under some kind of control I didn't know about and that all was well. Intellect doesn't control the sweat glands or the adrenals, though, and I was slippery with sweat and jittery with adrenaline, and tingling.

Abruptly I realized that my tingling was induced from an external source and that I'd been feeling it for some time. Now that tingle was building up to a resonance point in the meteor itself; the whole thing began ringing like a gong. The sound went on and on, and then tapered off into a tingle again.

I heard Cricket's calm voice speaking into the radio: "First resonance point."

Intellect got a little more control over the autonomic system then. Whatever landing procedure—landing a craft this size?—was in use, it was at least one familiar to those in charge. There was some faint hope in the back of my mathematical mind that we weren't about to be spread all over the inside of that chamber, irrational though my nerves tried to tell me the hope might be.

The R.A.I. began to show a distinct decline over the last few moments and was no longer tripping into the red. My gaze went to the nav scope.

The planetary image that it presented was roughly that of a half moon, with a terminator, probably the dawn line, almost directly beneath us. We were swinging into the night side.

As I watched, the progress of the terminator across the planetary disk slowed. There was still a bare line of light showing by the time it paused and moved slightly back. The main visible feature of the planet had become a lightning storm immediately beneath us.

The storm began to swell with our descent, and the intermittent flashes of lightning that had at first appeared to be a bar fanned out into a coil, a shaped funnel, beneath us. Again, my whole being was assaulted by the audible effect of the meteor in resonance with some external force. Then we were beneath the top of the storm and I could see that it was not a storm, but an orderly network of electrical flashes coiling around us and pulsing in an electronic dance that was followed by the sound in the ship itself as faithfully as though we were riding a loudspeaker.

The sound went on and on. The nav scope showed faint features of the planetary surface were becoming visible from much too close. The bowl-shaped horizon was swinging up and around us.

Then we were down. With only the faintest of jars. The altimeter read zero.

I must have been shaking and white as a sheet, but through my daze I heard Cricket's voice:

"Okay, ground control. We're down. Check ejection orientation."

"Ejection orientation is on target," the radio assured her. "Proceed with ejection."

I was trying to find my voice to ask Gallagher what the hell they were talking about, just for the relief of knowing there was a voice to hear, when a heavy blow slammed into the entire surface of my body. I was crushed under acceleration as though I were being launched by a primitive rocket.

Then we were falling. There was a distinct splash—a reorientation—and the control room settled into a quiet bobbing motion on its side. Gallagher, Cricket, and I were strapped to our

mats and couch against a wall. The controls
were on the floor. The bulkhead was the ceiling.

I stayed there shaking until the inner
bulkhead swung down and the handholds on its
outer surface were ready to serve as a ladder.

A voice called down, "Okay, you guys. You
can come out now."

Gallagher and Cricket had got themselves un-
strapped and were stepping carefully across the
controls. Me, I couldn't seem to find the buckles,
and with a giggle, our young captain reached
over and helped me unstrap as though I were a
typical passenger.

"Come on, big boy," she said. "Time to get
your ground legs working."

Gallagher heaved himself up the ladder, and
the whole cabin swayed in response to his motion. My feet nearly swayed out from under me.

"Steady as she goes," Cricket said, grabbing
my elbow. "We'll be out of this tube in a
minute."

I scrambled up the ladder and found a short
rope ladder above the hatch, leading to a walkway above.

The scene outside was arc lit, and I could see
that the walkway swung from a crane. Magnetic
grapples firmly secured the tiny tubular cabin,
now floating in a small body of water, to the
crane. The cabin in which we'd been traveling
looked scarcely more than an oversize piece of
stovepipe, tiny and inadequate, now.

The asteroid itself was nowhere in sight.

SIX

The taste of freedom is a heady thing. You could feel it in the air; you breathed it when you breathed. The place was alive with it. And you could see it in the technology around.

There's a difference when people are building things because they want to build them, and there aren't a batch of bureaucrats that have to argue the purpose and concept from a political or corporate standpoint for years before anything can be done.

There's a difference in the people, too. On Earth, you're a citizen of this or that and a member of this or that, but you speak of "they" when you speak of the factors that really control your life and your planet.

On Betsy Ann, every person there owned that planet. It was theirs. They didn't speak of *they*, they spoke of *we*. It has a different sound.

We were sitting in a workmen's canteen, on a rise about twenty kilometers from and overlooking the port. The port—or industrial complex. I don't know which you would call it.

I was over the shakes and beginning to understand the theory behind the method by which Betsy Ann was capable of landing not only asteroids of the size we'd come in on, but also interstellar ships, even if they are as delicate as eggs. I felt like a schoolboy. Impressed is hardly the word for it. I'd been expecting a primitive economy.

At that, it *was* a primitive economy in a way. It was spotty. There hadn't been time yet to tool up for consumer goods. But they were under way in directions Earth hadn't even dreamed of for generations.

The landing system was from what Gallagher called their *solar tap*. They were tapping the electrical potential that exists between a planet and its orbiting proton and electron belts—the belts of ionized particles caught in the planet's magnetic field.

The landing system was part of a power system that produced, from this one site, enough electricity to power the entire continent on a broadcast basis.

Broadcast power. It had been known on Earth since the days of Nicola Tesla—the system for putting power on the airwaves the way radio and TV are broadcast. Electric power that you could tune into, the way you tune in a radio.

With broadcast power, you didn't have to have wires strung around the continent to plug in motors and appliances and furnaces and the like. You didn't have to carry your own fuel in your ground car. You tuned in your motor to the power frequency, the way you tune in a radio to the frequency of the station you want to hear.

Earth hadn't had broadcast power, though she'd known how to broadcast it, because the production of power was geared to installations that didn't have sufficient potential that you could waste it on the airwaves. But the power potential in the solar tap was so great you could throw it away on an inverse-square basis and still be able to tune in at the coast lines, two thousand miles distant, and run anything you wanted to run, from a manufacturing complex to a skimmer.

The power that exists between the ground potential on any planet and the orbiting proton and electron belts trapped in the magnetic field of any planet, is fed by the solar wind of the sun around which the planet orbits, and it is a practically limitless potential. Electrons from the solar wind make their way in through the magnetic poles of the planet, distribute themselves at its crust, and seep through the insulating atmosphere towards the strong positive potential of the inner proton belt.

If you make a "short circuit" through the atmosphere by creating an ionized pathway with a laser beam that reaches to the ionosphere, the top of the insulating atmospheric layers, the electrons will jump across the short circuit, changing the groundside potential. When the groundside potential lowers, it makes it possible for more electrons to pour in from the solar wind to equalize the potential. The planet is effectively recharged, and you can short-circuit again.

It's done in milliseconds, and it's done on a pulse-basis. You turn the laser-beam short circuit off and on in an alternating-current effect, and it's most efficient at a low sonic frequency, although it has radio-frequency overtones.

There was a group of huge pyramidal structures that were the bases for the solar tap and landing system. A huge, central pyramid was the tap itself; built of granite with a marble overlay, and of sufficient size to insulate the tremendous bursts of power flow from the ground. The laser installation was on a small platform at the peak of the pyramid, and the control systems were centered well inside where the X rays and other radiation from the flow would not harm the technicians.

From this central pyramid, the pulsed power was broadcast across the continent, and even from inside the canteen and at this distance you could hear the deep-throated roar of that power, pulsing through at a frequency within the audible range. *Chee-ops, chee-ops, chee-ops,* it seemed to say as it shorted in, was cut off, and pulsed in again.

It was the landing system that used the smaller, satellite pyramids around the big one and that used other factors of the huge central pyramid as well.

The landing system was a gigantic web of laser beams, angled upward and focused to create a huge electrical discharge spiral that used magnetic induction and repulsion to bring the meteors in. They could bring in any metallic ship as well on that huge spiral, even though the interstellar ships were comparatively fragile; for the gentle cradle of the magnetic induction-propulsion system could raise or lower the gigaton masses as evenly as a freight elevator might bring down a crate of delicate electronic equipment.

The landing system. From the huge central pyramid, and from each of the smaller ones, two great alternating laser beams angled upward, aimed through tunnels internal to the pyramids and geometrically accurate to a hair. Those beams discharged their alternating spirals into a crisscrossed web of induction-repulsion that caught a ship and either stepped it up from rung to rung of the magnetic induction-propulsion ladder, or cradled it gently downward.

It was a magnificent sight, that solar tap landing system. As long as I was on Betsy Ann, I never ceased to be caught by tremendous awe and delight when it was turned on. It wasn't turned on now. Nothing was being landed or taking off. Only the one beam from atop the central pyramid pulsed its broadcast power and sang its deep-throated song. But I'd just ridden that ladder with its sure megaton grasp down from orbit, as gentle as a scientist's waldo handling a radioactive rabbit, and I was trying to understand the theory.

There were already central pyramids supplying power on each of the three continents of Betsy Ann, I was told. Those would soon be supplemented with satellite pyramids to create landing systems on each continent. Meanwhile, the equipment needed to convert Betsy Ann from a desert planet to a lush green one could operate anywhere on broadcast power.

"But why haven't they gotten this on Earth?" I finally asked.

"Stop-motion thinking," Gallagher answered. "Fear-thinking. Bureaucratic, cosmocorp, governmental thinking. Anyhow," he added, "earth's already built a steel-frame civilization and she'd have to use some real know-how to introduce a tap without frying people because of the resonance factor. It's best to stick with stone or plastic buildings when you're using a tap."

"But where's the meteor we came down in, and what's your plan for it?" I asked. "That's a big plenty of steel."

"Over there." He pointed to where I could see a glow in the sky at the center of the port complex. "We can use steel. We just use it with know-how."

I stared at the glow in the sky. "Surely it couldn't have been that hot?"

"That glow? That's not the meteor. That's the melting tap in operation. But the meteor did come in at a red heat, at least in its surface layers. You see, we land them direct into the furnace, and as soon as everybody's clear, they change the frequency of the induction current and start melting them down. Saves quite a bit of time, and time's our most precious commodity. The energy we're not worried about—that we've got in plenty. But it takes time to reheat, and if the ejection mechanism doesn't work, it's a couple or three hours' setback to lose the heat that was built up during descent so that we can get the people out. And then we have to reheat the darned thing so we can melt it down."

"Isn't that a rather expensive way to get steel?" I asked.

He grinned. "You're just not used to the idea of really planetary power," he said. "Those meteors—asteroids, really—can be brought in, melted down, and ready to use for tool steel at a cost per ton of, say, a hundredth of a solar credit."

"There are lots of corporations on Earth," Cricket interrupted, "that would gladly pay a hundred credits for that same ton. Delivered on Earth."

It was a strange, mixed-up economy, there on Betsy Ann. Broadcast electric power—a far development from the puny atomic power stations of Earth—yet we were sitting in the most primitive of cabins. A crude construction of logs laid together to surround a restaurant space, and heated from a rock stack that had a hole through the center and a lower opening into which you could thrust twigs and branches from the local trees to make a fire. Crude but comfortable, and I must admit that that open fire, which I got to know fairly well, was a cheerful thing to watch after the bleak warmth of a starship cabin.

Then, contrasted with the room and the open fire, the lighting system. Hollow fishbowls, or globes, approximately twelve centimeters in diameter, resting in metal brackets with no attachment whatsoever to the base, or of the base to wires of any sort. When you picked a globe from its bracket, the light dimmed and nearly went out, leaving only the glowing pattern of the fingers holding it. Heavy, of heavy glass, like a crystal ball; and filled with a low-pressure gas that was ionized by repeated bombardment with other ions excited by the higher harmonics of the broadcast-power frequency.

It was an odd contrast, the crudenesses and the advanced technologies side by side there on Betsy Ann. The people made an odd contrast, too. It was a matter of only a half hour or so before I found that I, a captain and a graduate engineer from Earth's best academies, was one of the more inept in some ways, though I did manage to shine in others.

Word spreads fast on a planet like Betsy Ann. When the first man wandered in, was introduced and joined us, I didn't think much of it. He was tall, stooped, and about forty. Dr. Strathmore, they named him, and the title rather surprised me. You don't expect doctors among wolves; but the question in my mind was just a passing thought, and he had me talking in minutes, asking questions with a voluble curiosity that was unexpected in a total stranger.

While we were talking, three others walked in; then a twosome; then three or four singles. They were all introduced, several of them as doctor this or that. I gave up trying to get the names straight. They were all firing questions about Earth conditions: whether there were any changes in attitude, what changes there had been in colonial trading policies (nothing but a stiffening of the old attitudes), and the like. The questions were coming so fast that I didn't have much time to think about the men doing the asking.

Then a rotund, bouncy sort of person walked in, and I recognized his face from the Tri-D even before he was introduced. Dr. Lamar

Jacobs. I began to feel unreal.

"But," I said, ". . . but you're a Ph.D. doctor. You're the head of the Institute of Astrophysics! You're in the Lunar Observatories!"

He smiled cheerfully. "Nope," he said, "I'm on Betsy Ann. Been here almost a year."

Gallagher was laughing, and his laughter rang through the small cabin, joined by the others. "You think these were all medical doctors?" he asked finally through his laughter.

"Of course," I said stiffly, then added, feeling myself getting red and embarrassed, "It did occur to me that you had quite a large complement of the medical profession here. But then, I don't know the size of your colony."

The colony had been growing. If you take the cork out of a bottle that's full of ferment, the ferment will spill out, and there's no use trying to stop it. Once Gallagher had founded an independent colony, the colonists began to arrive. How each one got there was a separate story; why each one got there was a separate story, too, except for the one thing they had in common: They wanted the privilege of working and living out from under.

Out from under what? Frustration. Secrecy. Regulation. Stalemate. Out from under the blanketing stop-motion, don't-move-without-permission, investigation-every-week, security-guarded policies of Earth science. Or politics. Or just plain daily living.

The ones who had come to debrief me and to find out what talents I might have that would prove useful—it was a while before I realized that that was what it was: a debriefing and talent-search session—were mostly scientists and engineers. But every type of person that goes to make up a civilization was represented in those who had found their way to Betsy Ann.

A few groups had even hijacked corporation ships on their way to other planets and made them detour by Betsy Ann. "We radio those to orbit one of the outer planets, and we meet them," Gallagher said.

Others got there by paying their way to a company planet and then getting word to Gallagher to pick them up on his next tour by.

"There's a sort of rule of thumb that we've found has worked out in which way people get here," Gallagher said. "If you're kind of conservative in your thinking—though most people wouldn't call it conservative to pick up and climb the wall out of Earth and into freedom—if you're a conservative independent, let's call it, you head for a planet and get word to me. But if you're crackling mad at the way civilization's grown on Earth and its tame planets, if you're a no-holds-barred, let's-get-out-there-and-see-what-we-can-make-happen type, if you're mad because the government and the corporations took over space—then you pirate a ship and make it head for Betsy Ann."

All the time, Cricket sat there as though she belonged, her freckle-faced little-girl pony-tail appearance belied by the ability with which she joined what was essentially technical conversation. Her light, bantering tone added as sparkling and warm a note to the surroundings as the glowing fishbowl lamps.

When the owner of the canteen came over, bringing a guitar, and handed it to her, the contrast was even stranger. She curled up, then, on the straight-backed chair in which she was sitting. Sort of curled over the guitar and forgot anybody else was around while she crooned to it, tuning it. It took them quite a while, the guitar and Cricket, to decide they were really where they wanted to be in tone and in time and in place, I guess. Meanwhile the conversation went on, slightly muted as though in respect to the guitar and its mistress.

Finally, not uncurling, just sort of opening the curl to include those of us at the table, Cricket began humming and strumming, and then, in a thin voice, quiet and so soft you had to reach for it, she began to sing:

Once upon a time, a rain fell from the sky
and washed out all the green and gold and
*   song. . . .*

I recognized the song, though I'd probably not heard it since I was a child. It had been a Protest song, written by a young Scotswoman somewhere between World War II and World War III; during the period known as the cold war, when atomic power meant atomic destruction. And then, belatedly, I recognized the name. Joinson.

It was a haunting melody; a haunting theme, and the chorus, as quiet as the rest, cut to my heart:

People said it wouldn't fall; others said they knew
*   the time would come . . .*
Some thought they'd play their game and never pay
*   the dues—*

> *But it doesn't really matter now the Earth lies
> cold—and gone.*

It was then, I think, that I despairingly fell in love with Cricket Joinson. Despairingly, because I realized I was hopelessly old-fashioned. Despairingly, because this was a modern world with modern technology, and I was Earth-bound in spite of Earth's rigid senilities. *Let's consider the value,* Gallagher had said, *and then we'll discuss the price.* All I'd been looking at all these years was the price, with no thought of the value. So I sat there feeling hopelessly out of the value because I had refused to pay the price.

Then I took myself to task mentally. They could have the freedom; but my job, I told myself severely, was to get back to Earth and to cram the facts of the colonies down the Space Commission's throat; to make them listen and change. I didn't say it aloud. I was quite sure they would laugh at me. But this, I felt, would be my contribution to the new civilization. When it had been made, and if I still felt the way I was beginning to feel, then perhaps I would have paid the price of entrance into Betsy Ann that I felt I must pay before I had the right to join them. And I would have paid the price in a manner that included a stubborn loyalty to Earth, no matter that it had shown itself to be muddleheaded, stupid, backward and intolerant.

So I continued to answer the questions as eagerly as they were asked, and my answers were all couched in the reasoning behind the muddleheadedness that they showed. I think the men questioning me were right impatient with that for a long time before Jim Strathmore finally spoke up.

It was right after I'd been making a full-fledged apologia for the colonial policies that made something like Stellamira possible. Strathmore leaned back in his chair and sort of took over the floor for the rest of them.

"Dundee," he said kindly, "stupidity always has its rationale. That makes it nonetheless stupid. Let me put it more strongly," he went on quietly. "Suicide always has its rationale. Its justifications. Its reasons. It's still suicide.

"Earth is committing suicide. We all know the rationale. We've all escaped from Earth. You can buy it and say, 'Poor, pathetic Earth is acting stupidly.' Or you can refuse it and say that if poor, pathetic Earth wants to be poor, pathetic Earth, the only way to stop the trend is to establish a terminal so strong that Earth has to forget suicide and get on with the business of competing.

"Now," he went on, "if Earth continues to commit suicide to the bitter end, well, it will be dead. But the race of man won't be dead because we're here. So, though we can't prevent the suicide of the planet, we can prevent the suicide of the race. And we're doing just that.

"If Earth wants to look up and notice that there's life to be lived and competition to be had, then she can get up off her sickbed and get back into the business of living and growing and being vital."

I was shocked. I hadn't thought of Earth as a

"poor, pathetic planet," though I may have thought of the crowded minions there, jammed in to the point where they had to be controlled in order not to step on each other, as poor, pathetic people. When Lamar Jacobs joined the diatribe to say that the poor, pathetic people of Earth were that way by their own refusal to change the situation, and that they were furthermore trying to create colonies of poor, pathetic people in their own image, I was inclined to agree with him.

I learned a lot that night, for all it was they who were debriefing me. I learned a lot in the next few weeks as well, and though one hijacked ship came through and I knew I could go out with the ferry and take passage back to Earth, I made excuses to myself and stayed on Betsy Ann.

Cricket ferried me around the planet on her various business that seemed to include a lot more than just piloting meteors. It was much later that I learned that she'd been shunted off her normal routines to go on errands for the purpose of ferrying me about. I guess Gallagher took more seriously than I thought my plans to report to Earth and wanted to be sure I'd make a full report.

I saw the Beta and Gamma tap stations. Since Betsy Ann is mostly desert, the most vital work I saw was where tap-powered machines were digging dams down into the desert sands to stop the water that's always seeping slowly from higher land beyond the desert to lower land wherever it may be, deep beneath any desert area. The dams force the water to the surface. Then growing things take hold and send down roots to keep the water at the surface, until the desert is no more. It was a huge grid of narrow, deep trenches that they dug down into the desert sands. Then they melted the sand they'd taken out and poured it—molten lava—in again, to form their dams.

I also saw the method by which they brought drinking water to the port and other centers. They froze ice ships at the poles and floated them down to the desert areas to melt there. To build an ice ship, they simply laid plastic forms where glaciers were melting into icy rivers and let them fill with water. Near the surfaces of the huge, streamlined forms, they used ice mice to create systems of tunnels just under the surface through which brine could be pumped at below the temperature of freezing water.

They cast motors into the ships as well—motors and controls. Then, in the dead of winter, when the streamlined forms were thoroughly frozen, they started pumping the brine through the tunnels to prevent melting, and they started the motors and took those ice ships nearly a quarter of the way around the planet to haul them out and let them melt where the water was needed. It was a far less expensive method than desalinating briny sea water.

But it was the Jacob's Ladder landing system of the big Alpha tap that held me fascinated. When it went into operation at night, the faint play of lights that were the melting tap would dim and pale for a period of perhaps two

minutes; and the glow lamps of the area went
nearly out as well.

Then the horizon would light up again, and
instead of the pale single streamer that flickered
in the tap's regular pulsing, instead of the om-
nipresent *chee-ops, chee-ops* that was the deep-
throated song of the tap in its normal operation,
the huge, ladderlike structure of beams would
flame into the sky, and the chorus of the other
pyramidal structures would join into a deep sub-
sonic roar like the afterrumble of thunder, in-
terspersed with overtone harmonics that were
more like a drum than the oboe note of the single
tap. *Angkor-watt, angkor-watt, angkor-watt.*

On the flaming ladder crisscrossed against the
dark, a darker mass would slowly make its way;
a giant figure stepping up in improbable
smoothness, lifted by the powerful chorus of
light and sound, until it reached the top of the
ladder, a bright point in the sunlight that was
shining up there. Then its trajectory would
curve, and it would sweep off and away, out of
sight.

It had a pull to it, that ladder; a pull that was
as strong as space itself, and as irresistible. I
longed to be out in the starways, to climb those
golden rungs and fling myself into the freedom of
space. The sight of that tap was a powerful long-
ing for the farther stars, and the farther . . . to
infinity, perhaps. It was an unreasoning reaction. Safety is on a planet; space is dangerous.
But . . . but the pull of that ladder is a deeper
pull than any security can withstand. I knew I
would be going out again.

Once, when I'd stood enmeshed in the powerful web as it lifted a ship out to the stars until sight and sound of it were long since gone, and the low, pulsing beat of the *angkor-watt, angkor-watt* had been replaced by the oboe-sonic *chee-ops* of the single tap, I turned to find Cricket beside me, staring not at the tap, but at me. There was a look on her face. I took her in my arms, oblivious of the canteen and the people in the canteen.

"You'll go with me?" I asked. "I have to go."

Her voice against my chest was muffled. "Not to Earth," she said. "Not to Earth for any purpose."

I let her go then. A man has a purpose and he must serve that purpose. But I felt a loss as great as the loss when the ladder dies and you're still on a planet, gravity-bound.

Ships were going out to Refuge now with some regularity. Most of the trading was one-way, with Betsy Ann sending hand tools and manufactured parts and the like, and accepting Refugian scrip which was actually valueless except as an IOU, for they'd not had time to produce a return-trade ability. Yet the returning ships were carrying things needed on Betsy Ann, and I learned that the black-market traders in the colonies were accepting those Refugian IOUs at nearly face value, despite the fact that Refuge would pay off Stellamira as its first priority.

That spoke a lot for Gallagher and for the heady feeling that was permeating the starways. I think the Refugian scrip was actually considered of better long-term value than that of the company colonies. Those who could were banking it for the future.

It was a pride that was pervading the starways, and that's a yeasty thing.

Gallagher was not handling the trade now. Betsy Ann had its own ships, and though they could trade only on the black market, for company rules were strict about no trading with the "outsiders," the black market was flourishing. The traders knew the dangers and impossibilities of that market; but, like the privateers of history, there were ways, and the ways were found.

Gallagher was still on Betsy Ann, though I saw little of him and actually forgot to ask what he was about. Forgot—or didn't feel I had the right.

So I was both surprised and pleased when he walked into the canteen one night while Cricket and I were having coffee, just back from one of her business trips.

"The *Glacier*'s setting course for Durango," Gallagher said briefly and without greeting.

I felt the smile on my face freezing. I felt out of it. I had been excusing myself from finding a way to Earth, but my course was set. I had set that course myself, I told myself, and I couldn't deviate.

Then I held my longings firmly in check, and I held my voice light and bantering, while I said, "Thought you'd forgotten all about Durango, Dublin."

He looked at me queerly. "When you set a goal," he said finally, slowly, "you can rush the goal and lose. Or you can take your time and make your plans and get them ready. That gives you a good chance. I've been tooling up," he said.

"If you'll have me," I heard myself answering, "I'm going along." I felt rather than heard Cricket let out a sigh, and it could have been one of relief. I don't know.

Gallagher looked from me to her and back to me. "Thought you were course-set for Earth and the Space Commission," he said.

I guess that's when I first took a good look at what I was doing and why. I hardly recognized my own reasoning nor even my voice. I was sort of watching at a great distance a change taking form that had already taken place.

"When a man's trying to commit suicide," I heard myself say quietly, "you can let him have the right to do as he sees fit. Or you can pay the price of trying to talk him out of it, and then trying to get him to rebuild his life; and then trying to get him to be worth a damn. Or you can go find the busy people who have the courage not to knuckle under to the hazards of being alive, and you can join them to build a vital life yourself, with them. They're the people of courage—and it's courage that's worth backing and being with and being part of. But it takes that courage on your part, too. You can be the victim of the poor, pathetic, courageless yokel while you tell yourself you're a do-gooder—or you can be the partner of the people that have sense and guts, if you've got sense and guts.

"I think," I said slowly, "that I've got sense

and guts, though it's right late showing. If you think so, too, I'll go along."

I stopped then, but there was a silence. The silence continued, so finally I went on.

"There's the price of anything," I quoted Gallagher slowly, quoted him from way back where he might not remember, but perhaps he'd recognize his own logic. "And then there's the value. I got sort of fooled about the value, or maybe I wanted to be fooled. The price is pretty high. But I think I'll opt for the value and pay the price, if I can find a way to make the trade."

Then it was that Gallagher threw back his head and laughed, a loud, happy, deep laugh that had a satisfying ring to it. Cricket was laughing, too, with tears sparkling in her eyes as she laughed.

And I sat there trying to see what was funny. It didn't seem funny to me at all—just a matter of pride and value, and a high price to pay that I knew would be a high price.

Gallagher rose, still laughing, and he looked down at me kindly; and though I almost resented the look, it was pleasurable deep inside.

"We lift in two hours," he said. "You two won't need to bring anything except a few clothes. Heavy-duty clothes," he added. "Boots and fieldwear." Then he turned and left.

SEVEN

It's a strange phenomenon, this thing the psych boys call déjà vu. I've never had it before or since. But during the time we spent on Durango, it occurred again and again. Maybe it was just continuous.

It was as though I had been there before—doing the same thing at the same time and in the same places over and over again, to the point where I knew what was happening just before it happened.

I seldom had any feeling that I wanted to interfere with what was going on; but even at the times when I did want to and did interfere, it was as though I'd done it before and was destined to do it again. Like watching yourself in a hall of mirrors doing the same things back as far as you can see.

Durango was one of the more settled planets, by a matter of three or four generations. It had small but thriving cities, and a compromise situation between the company cities and the independents that broke out into open warfare on occasion, but that was mostly quiescent hostility. I guess it was like the relationship between England and the American colonies way back when.

The company "owned" the planet by right of grant from the Space Commission, so it had the "right" to tax and to police the planet. But the colonists of the second, third, and fourth generations were no longer indentured servants—only the new colonists that were brought in were that —because even Earth couldn't make it stick that a son owed the debts of his father.

Perhaps they could have made even that father-to-son indebtedness stick on a planet like Stellamira, where the planet itself is so hostile that the colonists can't escape to the Outback. But Durango was a pleasanter planet, and although the Outback was extremely hazardous, it was not unlivable.

Durango was like the early American colonies in a lot of senses. Earth wanted to keep the colonies as sources of raw materials and to reserve to herself the right of manufacture. Durango would have been much better off to go into manufacture to supply her own needs, but it wasn't permitted. Oh, handmade stuff and that sort of thing, yes. But tooling up for real manufacture— no. Taxes took care of that and were set with that purpose in mind. When an independent avoided taxes, he could be put in jail. So the equation worked.

It was a subtle equation, as those equations are. By law, the independents who had won their way free of any indebtedness to the company and preferred to support themselves rather than work for the company, had the full free right to do so. They were equal under the law and were taxed on the same basis that company employ-ecs were taxed. Of course, the company salaries were set to take care of the taxes, and the taxes, which were paid to the company itself, were deducted before the salaries were paid. The taxes made any independent industrialization prohibitively expensive; and if it was necessary to send a small army to put a man or men in jail for avoidance of taxes, it was still a "police action."

The same system worked to stifle any trading by the independents. By the books, it was a free-trade economy. An independent shipper could land and take off and had the same rights as any company shipper. Even the tariffs paid on goods shipped were the same. But since the company "owned" the planet and collected the tariffs, though those tariffs were prohibitive to an outsider, they were a matter of taking money from one pocket to put it in the other to the company. There was also the question of red tape, which could be cut or snarled at company convenience.

Gallagher and I landed at the port (Cricket stayed with the *Glacier*), and true enough, we were free to land. The planetary control signaled in our lander just as they would signal in a company lander.

Then came the red tape, and it wasn't too surprising that it was snarled, if you knew what you were looking at. There were forms to fill and more forms, and then a frozen-in-ice little blonde who insisted on questioning everything we said, and cross-questioning the answers, and asking our motives and countermotives and counter-countermotives for landing on the planet to the point where I felt like screaming at her.

It was like talking to a primitive computer—one that seemed to keep losing track of what it was talking about. I finally realized, after a few hours, that the little blonde's program read something like: "Keep them talking until Intelligence sends further instructions." Evidently Intelligence needed plenty of time for whatever it was deciding, or checking, or planning.

It went on for about eight hours in all, and then was over as abruptly as though the red tape and confusions hadn't been growing by the minute. In the middle of one of Gallagher's more involved sentences, the blonde computer suddenly rose and left the room. She returned after about five minutes.

"You are both free of the port, but will not be allowed to go farther," she said in her best iceberg manner. "Captain Gallagher has been extended a week's visitor's permit for trading.

"You, Captain Dundee, are another problem. We have been advised that you are wanted for desertion and piracy by the U.N. Space Commission and the government of Stellamira. We seriously advise you to go to the local Space Commission, arrange a hearing, and get the matter settled. That, however, is up to you. The Space Commission has no local authority and cannot seize you while on this planet, nor has Durango any local charges against you. What will happen when you return to space I have neither the knowledge nor authority to say. However, you also have a week's visitor's permit, and should you wish to extend that permit, such an extension will probably be made contingent upon your settling your problems with the local Space Commission agents."

"Well," said Gallagher happily, "it seems we've got a week here, Harald. All I really wanted to do here was to go over to Suzie's Place, anyhow. Why don't you come along with me while you decide what to do about the Earthie charges?"

I rose stiffly and nodded. "Sounds like sense to me," I said. "Perhaps I'd better investigate my rights a bit before I walk into the compound where the Space Commission has jurisdiction. I'll clear those charges," I added grimly, for the idea of the charges had been eating into me whether I knew them for a batch of lies or not. "It's the legal technicalities of the clearing that are the moot point."

Perhaps half of that was for the benefit of the iceberg and anyone else that was listening. But half of it was for myself, and that deep something in me that still believed that justice could be done in even so highly political a situation as the one I'd gotten embroiled in. I knew for a fact that it couldn't, but there's something stubborn in a man that believes long after he knows what isn't so.

It was a grimy, down-at-the-heels port town, far different from Stellamira because of the differences in planetary hostility. It was more spread out, and the company areas were not so strictly divided from those of the colonists. The segregation here was more from the fact that company officials lived in large places on the outskirts and the colonists in town. There were no ghetto walls. Crossing a street could take you from one area into the other. The differences were obvious, but the street was the division point.

Suzie's place was in the center of town, but this time it was an all-colonist establishment. It was early evening, and a neon sign over swinging doors proclaimed that the place was open for business. From out on the street you could hear the sound of a tinkling piano and of raucous conversation and laughter.

We pushed through the swinging doors and spotted Suzie by the piano. Gallagher waved at her grandly, then galloped across to where she stood, swung her up like a prize chicken, and bussed her roundly. I stood back and waited. When he'd set her down, she turned to me and gave me a warm kiss on the cheek. Then she turned back to Gallagher.

"So you've decided to forget that I hijacked your ship into a small detour?" she asked him loudly, without the slightest hint of apology.

He bowed from the hips. "When a lady wishes to be taxied to the place of her choice, who am I to do other than see to it that her wishes are obeyed?" he said with a grin. "But the hire of the taxi must be paid, and I've come to collect my fare."

With that he picked her up unceremoniously and headed up the stairs with her. Suzie gave him a few little kicks of token protest, but was obviously pleased.

I didn't know what was expected of me, but I didn't have long to wonder. One of the girls, the

one who'd been on a crutch at Stellamira and
who still walked with a slight limp, appeared at
my elbow and offered me a drink. We made our
way to the bar. I took the drink and played with
it, and we made polite conversation. It was made
clear to me that a trip upstairs would be available, but I refused that and continued to play
with my drink.

Then each of the girls in turn made an excuse,
one time or another, to come and sit beside me.
Though I offered to buy them drinks, I was
made to understand that the hospitality of the
bar was mine. We chatted rather inanely, for we
never mentioned Stellamira nor Betsy Ann; just
light conversation that seemed quite unreal. I
found myself more than just fond of each and
every one of them. We couldn't mention it, but
we'd been through a war together, and there was
a bond we could feel as we sat side by side; a
bond that I held with each of them while we
talked inanities and smiled rather pasty smiles.
It's funny about that bond. Their profession,
even if it had been only a profession, made no
difference; their makeup and their crudities, for
they were not uncrude, made no difference. The
bond was there, and we could feel it; and each of
us knew the loyalties inherent in that bond were
permanent; that we were all members of a tribe
that could be joined in no other way than the
way it had been formed.

Even so, it was a long wait, and I may have
grown a trifle nervous, though I sat outwardly
calm and feeling warm with the bonds. I am new
at the business of revolution, and I feel chancy

about that business. As I sat at the bar, my back began to feel naked, and the hairs at the nape of my neck felt stiff and standing. I felt watched by cold eyes. I was sure that there were company spies in the room.

When Gallagher finally came down, he was obviously tipsy. Having played with the one drink all evening, I was sober, and I had assumed that he, too, would be careful. Evidently I'd underrated his reactions to seeing Suzie again. I was furious, but I hid it well.

"Come along, Harald," he said jovially, swatting me on the back so hard that I swayed over the bar with the blow. "Come along, for the hour is early yet, and we've a bit of pub crawling to do before the night is out."

I rose, unsteady from the blow, and grasped his arm. "Perhaps we'd best go back to the lander for a bit of sleep first?" I suggested, low-voiced and cautious.

He threw his head back and laughed with a bellow that turned every head in the room. "Go back to bed, and me so long away from the spacelanes? Me so cramped yet from the months of settling in colonists who are serious and sober and God-fearing? Why, no, Harald. You go beddy-bye if that is to your liking, but me, I thought to see the town. Maybe even beard the Company Governor in his lair." He leered down into my face, and I became really worried, for he was obviously very far in his cups.

But I'd not desert him, and we made our way boisterously to the street. He stopped everyone we passed to exchange a greeting or to gainsay an offer of a drink.

On the street, he took me by the arm and led me through the main part of the town. By now I knew that we were being followed.

I made it my policy to steer Gallagher to the most brightly lighted spots; I'd more than a suspicion that the company goons who were following us had nothing better in mind than getting us into a dark alley and leaving our bodies to be found there as though from a street fight. But it became more and more obvious as we tipsied our way along that this town was full of dark alleys. The joints you could visit were getting scarcer, and with more and longer stretches of dark pavement between.

Then, with a great shout, Gallagher dragged me off the main thoroughfare.

"'Tis Tiny's place we're forgetting," he said as he headed me up one of the darkest alleys we'd yet passed. If I'd a mind to struggle, the iron grip on my arm and a quiet hiss, "Come on now, Harald, play up," overrode it.

We were into the alley before I'd quite gathered my wits.

As the darkness surrounded us, Gallagher's tipsy gait left him, and he moved like a cat.

"Hold this over your nose," he whispered, and thrust a square of greasy cloth into my hand.

The greasiness caused my hand to hesitate on the way to my nose, and I was almost too late following his instructions. There was the faintest of tinkles behind us, near my heels, and a faint hiss. I forced the square of cloth, greasy or no, firmly over not only my nose, but my mouth.

It seemed anticlimactic then that we strolled on at a reasonable, unexcited pace, then stopped and waited scarcely ten meters from the entrance. I was about to take the cloth from my mouth and ask Gallagher what was happening when a half dozen figures appeared in the mouth of the alley, backlighted from the street beyond.

Cautiously, as though feeling their way, searching and unsure, the men came into the narrow way after us—and then began to disappear, dropping one by one.

I'd not been noticing Gallagher's faint count. ". . . and five and six. Okay. That took care of them, but there's more of them outside." His voice was low. "They didn't all come in. By now they'll have the other end of this alley sealed up, too."

You could touch the walls on each side of the narrow way by stretching, and Gallagher did just that, feeling along until he reached a door on his left. He centered on the door and then began scrabbling with his fingers along the pavement at his feet. Abruptly, he began heaving on something, whispering at the same time, "Give me a hand."

I moved beside him just in time to catch hold of the rim of a manhole cover. The two of us heaved it up and balanced it on edge next to the hole.

"Down you go."

My feet found the rungs of a ladder, and I made my way halfway down, then reached back a hand to support the lid as Gallagher moved onto the ladder beside me. Then we carefully replaced the lid over the hole.

"Safe to breathe yet?" I asked softly.

"Keep the cloth over your nose awhile longer. I used strong stuff. We've got to move quickly now, for they'll be all over that alley in another fifteen minutes. The gas may hold 'em off that long."

We felt our way down the blackness of a tunnel scarcely a man's height. The wires, pipes, and various panel boxes that my fingers passed over told me its usage.

Then ahead of us there was light, and the passage broadened into a dimly lighted underground room.

"Junction terminal," Gallagher said succinctly. I was about to move ahead when he held me back. "It'll have personnel relays in it," he said. "I hadn't time to get hold of the necessary electronics to knock them out."

We paused only a few meters from the lighted room, and I was thinking whether it would be wise to go back. Apparently Gallagher was thinking of something else, for a small flame appeared in his hand, and he began carefully tracing some of the cables that ran along the wall beside us.

"This should do," he decided with the air of a man talking to himself, as his other hand came out of his pocket holding a small knife. He made short work of slicing through the protective plastic cover and picking out a couple of the color-coded wires beneath. These he peeled carefully without breaking. Then he twisted them together.

"That'll give them enough to worry about for a while," he said in a satisfied tone of voice.

"How do you know you didn't just short out somebody's telephone?" I asked.

"Advantage of being a floating engineer," he answered. "I spent a couple of months working on this underground system between space hops once. That's when I got to know the problems here on Durango. I have just shorted out the intruder alarms that will tell the Powers That Be that every warehouse in this neighborhood, as well as all the tunnels and other guarded areas, have been invaded. We just became an army," he said, grinning.

"But won't that mean they'll have people swarming all over these tunnels looking for intruders?"

"Not a chance. They'll search the warehouses first. Then, in about ten or fifteen hours, they may find out exactly what happened. But come on—I'm not that sure that we've got that long."

There may have been a plan and pattern to the tunnel system that was undoubtedly logical and easily remembered by anyone who ever worked on it. But for me, it was a matter of walking and crawling, twisting and turning. Eventually there was another manhole cover. We heaved it out of our way and crawled into another alley.

"Took you long enough," said a nearby feminine voice, and there, leaning out the door of her skimmer, was Suzie. Seth was at the wheel. Gallagher replaced the manhole cover and piled in, with me right after him.

The skimmer took off, slowly at first, turning and twisting through areas of fewer and fewer

houses until we were away from the town. Then
Seth threw it into high-speed operation. I turned
to Gallagher.

"The company was just hoping we'd go back
to our lander," he told me happily. "If they
didn't have it booby-trapped, I don't know company minds. They want us dead, but they want
us dead unofficially. When we didn't head right
back for it, they decided to take further action,
but there's enough independence in this town
that they didn't want to be too open about it.
Then, too, we had to take the heat off Suzie's
Place by being long gone from there before we
disappeared."

"But if they've got our lander," I felt the fool
asking, because I thought I already knew the answer, "how the devil are we going to get out of
here?"

"That's what's been worrying a lot of people
for the last few years," Suzie answered me.
"We've got some independence, some of us; and
we've got parts of the planet more or less under
control. But how to get on and off—well, that's
gotten more difficult every week since the
Stellamira uprising. The port's free, theoretically—but time after time, independents
have had accidents at that port. And there's
nothing goes through it that the company
doesn't know about."

"But if you've got ground control—"

"Ground control means you control an *area*.
But the company controls the *space around* that
area. Anytime they've a mind to, they can drop
something on one of our installations, and who's

to say it wasn't an accident? Controlling the ground and being able to use it—well, those are two different things."

And that, I had to admit, was logical. I could get the picture. One independent every twenty square miles, the company wouldn't bother about. But let's see you set up a city under those conditions. Or even a good-sized farm.

It worked out to a standoff because the company couldn't use the planet either. With two and a half million independents scattered around, there wasn't a safe thing the company could do; any more than there was a safe thing the independents could do.

It was the old stalemate between ground-based guerrillas and an air-based opposing power. A setup where nobody can win unless one side can wear the other down, man by man, while the planet itself gets ground into the dust.

I've moved around a bit groundsides on some planets, but this was my first time on Durango; and it was actually the first time that I'd ever covered any really large distances in a ground vehicle. Not that you can call the skimmers ground vehicles, because they're not. They float along a few feet above the ground, and for a reasonable driver going a reasonable distance they make reasonable speed—say thirty to seventy kilometers an hour. They're quite capable of slowing down and threading their way through almost any rough country.

But in all my experience, I've never had a ride like the one I had that night. Seth drove with a sure control that was beautiful to watch, and I soon got over thinking of him as the stumble-word slow-wit I'd remembered him to be. But at our speed, even sure control wouldn't be enough, unless he knew the country like the palms of his hands.

The upper speed limit of a souped-up skimmer on a straight run over a flat plain is reputed to be some five hundred kilometers an hour, though no one in his right mind would drive half that fast on anything rougher than a mirror.

Actually, I had very little way of knowing how fast we were going; but from the sways, bumps, and bounces as we passed over various objects hidden in the darkness, I knew we were going far faster than any skimmer trip I'd made before.

Then we straightened out and slipped into a river. Or I should say over a river, for a skimmer never touches the water. And here Seth really let it out.

How far or how fast we traveled that night I don't know, but the next morning we were well into a range of mountains that are not even visible from the port—and we had gotten there over totally unimproved territory.

There was a tiny cabin that we got to just at dawn, and there we stayed. I'd thought it was a stopover point when we first arrived, but it turned out not to be. It was to be our head-quarters, I discovered, from which we were going to organize this revolution.

At least, it would be headquarters for me. For Gallagher and Suzie and Seth, it would be headquarters when they were there. Mostly they weren't there.

I was put in charge of creating an intelligence

system out of whatever ragtags and bobtails of independents could be spared from what I gathered was the main organization of guerrilla fighters. Where those fighters were concentrated, or what their plans were, it was decided best that no one knew who was not directly concerned. Should my intelligence members or I be captured, we could not give away what we did not know.

It *was* ragtag and bobtail, but the men, women, and even teeners who came to me for duty were more the sort of Betsy Ann than of the port town, so by comparison with those they'd be spying on, they were a top crew. Backwoodsy types. Rough. Most of them had contacts in the "cities" (little more than would have been termed towns on Earth); and some of them were not known to be Independents. Those last were given the most hazardous task of going back to live in the towns and to relay information. The others would be relays and would glean as many facts as they could from their contacts.

It is surprising how much information you can get, if you accept it in bits and piece it together into a pattern. Anything at all was fodder to our mill. The fact that some Joe had been transferred from one job to another. The bit that a cargo of such and such a size and weight, heavily guarded, had arrived. The number of uniforms to be seen on the streets on a given evening. The drunkenness or soberness of the company guards. The number and caliber of prisoners in the jail at any one point . . . Bits and pieces of information, each relatively meaningless in itself, that in the aggregate formed a pattern and a picture. We had one man in the police skimmer pool and one in planetary radar. They were invaluable.

We always knew in advance when a raid into Independent territory was scheduled, and we always managed to pinpoint the focus of the raid. Only once were we mistaken, and though I kept the fact to myself, I decided the raid had been diverted to another focus intentionally by a feint from Gallagher and Suzie's forces. Two hours before the raiders were scheduled to take off, word went around the port town like wildfire that there was a concentration of Independents up to something in a completely different direction, and the raid was refocused. A huge battle ensued, but I had no way of knowing whether our forces got off lightly or with heavy damage. Certainly our reports showed that the raiders suffered losses which, according to indications, were fairly heavy.

Gallagher and Suzie were seldom there. When they were, it was to drain me of all the information I could give them, with both of them keeping their mouths shut for fear of giving me information, and me doing my best to throttle my own inquisitiveness. They were quite right that what I didn't know couldn't be gotten out of me by drugs or torture, and they were quite right that if my intelligence system were traced and I were captured, I'd be subject to both. So I kept my curiosity to myself and even tried not to overhear when they were careless.

It was mostly Seth who acted as information

liaison, and I guess I was as sure as Suzie that no drugs and no tortures could get it out of him. Besides his absolute loyalty, he just plain wasn't good enough at organizing his thoughts into speech.

About two and a half months later, while I was thoroughly engrossed in the business of gathering data and drawing a picture of company activities on the planet, I got two pieces of news that scared the bejesus out of me. Either one of them would spell the end of us and our revolt, I felt; the combination spelled the end in terms so certain that there was no question in my mind.

Ships were landing and taking off at the port with regularity. I was reporting them, their cargoes in and out, and their personnel. But this was something different, and it wasn't at the port.

One of my most reliable runners came in with word that a strange craft had been seen in the Outback. It had been near the areas where I knew, trying not to know, that Gallagher and Suzie were operating.

It was a silent vehicle and literally huge, nearly two hundred meters in length with a shape like a stingray, according to my runner. It had come slowly drifting out of a cloud bank and had silently progressed up the valley. He had had confirmation from at least a dozen good sources, and all the descriptions were nearly the same.

With something like what he described, the companies would inevitably get the upper hand, I felt sure. Skimmers we could handle. The normal fliers that both company and Independents used were a problem, but we had those under control. But this? How do you combat a breakthrough in technology?

Word of this had to get to Gallagher at once. I debated sending the runner on to him, thought better of it, and decided to go myself. But before I got to the skimmer, I heard another skimmer coming in, and I waited.

There were five of them, flying heavy, but Seth's was in the lead so I knew it was all right. Then I saw that Gallagher was driving the second skimmer, and knew I could report direct to him. Suzie was driving the third. But when I saw who was driving the fourth skimmer, I ran to where she'd pulled up beside the cabin and opened the door for Cricket.

She spilled out into my arms. It may have been quite a while before I was thinking again.

Then, hanging on to Cricket's hand, I dragged her to where Gallagher, Seth, Suzie, and a man I didn't know were unloading hundreds of cartons, and I began to tell them about the new craft.

I was falling over my words, reporting, trying to get the detail of it to him, when I finally noticed that Gallagher was barely listening. I took a big grip on myself, dropped Cricket's hand, and got between Gallagher and the skimmer he was unloading.

"You've got to listen," I said. "This is important."

He smiled at me then. "Yes," he said. "It's important. It just happens we already know about it. I didn't mean to be impolite."

"Well, then, for God's sake, tell me what it is," I said desperately.

"Why, it's a new kind of landing craft. For landing people and freight from interstellar ships," he said. "Far more efficient than the landers we've been using."

"It's too big," I said flatly.

"It's two hundred and twenty-eight meters long," he told me. "And it can carry one hell of a lot of freight and equipment."

"It can't be a lander." There was doubt in my voice now, though I knew that a vehicle that size, flying around in the air and making little or no noise, couldn't possibly be a vehicle that could be launched with an inertial drive. All the book learning and all the training and all my background in space and space technology were telling me that Gallagher was either fooled or lying.

"Why, man," I said, "a vehicle that size couldn't even get up to Mach One in air, without blowing the planet half apart from the shock wave. How could it possibly be a landing craft?"

Gallagher looked at me solemnly, for all the world like a stupid student who's looked in the back of the book and is being smug about knowing the answers. "Don't have to go over Mach One," he said softly. "It's an L.T.A."

I must have looked blank, for he went on, "Lighter than air. It floats."

"Like a balloon?" I asked inanely.

"Yep. It's an adaptation of something they used to call a dirigible. And it's got a cruising altitude in excess of eighty thousand feet. But it's also got a drive that's good enough to take it away from the planet once it gets up that high."

"I've got a man in the radar setup," I said. "He'd have known it when a different type of lander was coming in. He watches for things like that."

"That radar's blind," Gallagher said. "No offense. All radars are set up to be blind to their preconceived notions of what can't be there. When people build radars to spot things coming in, they 'know'—at least in theory—the approximate range of speed that an object must have in order to do what they expect it to do. So, as good engineers, and in order to cut down on noise and false signals in their radar gear, they set up rejection circuits that reject things that aren't moving in the proper range of velocity. Therefore they literally didn't see it."

I could have gone on questioning Gallagher as long as he'd have let me, but it was at this point that the real blow fell.

A skimmer came in over the hills, and Suzie and Gallagher ducked inside the hut. It skidded to the ground and I headed toward it. The hatch opened and Jane, the girl with the limp, jumped out and came toward me as fast as she could move.

"Earth's sending a shipload of Space Marines," she called, panting.

I turned to call Gallagher, but he and Suzie were already running toward us.

"When?" he asked.

"They got word to me at Suzie's Place last night. It's already lifted from Earth. I got away as soon as I could. Nobody knows why, but the gossip is that you've been in the Outback so long, and Stellamira was so drastic, that the U.N.'s going to take a hand in settling the matter. The excuse is that Durango has been plagued with outlaw raids and has asked the Space Commission for assistance in subduing the outlaws."

Gallagher looked grim. Suzie was standing back with a waiting look on her face. Cricket must have come up while I wasn't noticing, for now she slipped her hand into mine.

"What are we going to do?" I asked, trying to keep the hopelessness out of my voice.

"What *you* are going to do," Gallagher said fiercely, "is to change your intelligence network over into a distribution network as fast as it can be done." He waved back to where Seth and the other man were still unloading the skimmers. "Get these items to every man jack of an Independent you can get them to. They came in on the L.T.A. lander you spotted, and we've got them now, but they've got to get to where they'll do us some good. By the time your men get these distributed, there will be more. You've got a week. Then I'll come get you."

Jane looked at Gallagher. Her face was strained and tired. "What's my job?" she asked.

"Take a load of these—all you can carry—to Suzie's Place," he said.

Then he, Suzie, and Cricket ran to the skimmers from which the last of the packages had just been unloaded, and they took off.

I felt empty, looking after them. Empty, and

with that sense of déjà vu haunting me. This had happened and would happen and was happening. There was nothing I could do about it except to follow the pattern as it was set.

I walked slowly over to the piles of packages. There were three kinds: A huge pile—nearly two-thirds of the lot—of one kind. A smaller pile —nearly one-third—of a second kind. A very small pile of the third.

I opened one of the cartons from the big pile, and relief flooded me as I pulled out one of the tiny guns that it contained. The thing fitted my hand as though it were tailored to me. It had the sort of beauty that comes from precision parts intricately fitted together into an overall pattern of purpose. It wasn't one of those gentle little water-pistol shockers that the colonists had constructed on Stellamira. This was lethal—from its optical surfaced muzzle to its palm-fitting trigger arrangement.

I carefully slipped it into my pocket and went to the second pile. Those cartons held communicators. Thousands of them. I didn't even pull one out. I knew without examining them that they solved most of the problems of my information network.

I turned to the small third pile, and when I opened a carton, I think my heart broke. They contained globes, each one with a built-on metal bracket—the lamps that could be powered only by broadcast power. Could be powered only by a solar tap.

Once I'd seen the globes I didn't have to pull the gun from my pocket to know that it, too, was a broadcast-power device. Nor the communicators. Though I did test one of each.

So the corporations had discovered solar taps and were about to turn one on. So we'd captured some of their supplies and wouldn't be caught completely flat-footed when it happened. So they still had the strength of us.

I stared at the globes, and I felt the massive power of Earth as though it were sitting on my shoulders compared with the puny bits of us that thought of ourselves as Independents. In that minute, the chances of our outlasting the might of Earth seemed to me miserably small.

EIGHT

That sense of déjà vu came on strongest a week later, when, alerted by some sixth sense, I jerked from the papers I was working on in the cabin about twilight and, abruptly worried, ran outside.

It came on strongest, and then it disappeared. Life was new and fresh and exciting again.

The L.T.A. lander, the dirigible-type stingray-looking vessel I'd heard described, hung about a hundred meters away, not six meters off the ground, with Gallagher climbing down a rope ladder from an underslung cabin in its middle, and eight men from it hawsering it to trees.

It was a huge craft, and hauntingly familiar. Not the replay type of familiarity I'd had before, but like an old friend come back. Yet it was a strange vehicle. Seen from this distance it was extremely thin, saucerlike; but seen from underneath, after I got there, it had a delta-shape and tail arrangement that gave it the stingray feel. Nearly as wide as its 228-meter length. It was an oddly shaped craft. The tautness of its hawsers told of its readiness to move off into the air, as though it were temporarily trapped in a spider's web, but yearning to be free.

I was still gawking when Gallagher reached ground. "Time to go now, Harald," he said.

I shook my head. "You may do as you like since you seem to have captured the means to do it. And I hope you're taking Cricket with you. But I've helped start something here, and just because they've gotten ahead of us, I'm not about to run like a scared rabbit. Unless," I asked hopefully, "everybody else on our side can run, too?"

Gallagher shook his head. "Damn it! The Earthie cruiser will be landing Space Marines in a couple of days now. We've got things to do meantime. Take my word for it—we're not running like scared rabbits. I haven't time to argue. Come along!"

I came. He wouldn't even let me go back to the hut for the papers I'd drawn up with the latest info. "You have everything we'll need in your head," he said as he practically shoved me up the ladder.

Cricket was in the control room. That fact registered, and I'm surprised that I registered anything else for a minute, but I did. Suzie was there, too. Soon Seth and seven other men who had been helping him loose the lander appeared, and I realized we were rising. Rising? The craft surged away from the ground like a thing alive, but so gently I could have stood on tiptoe and balanced with the greatest of ease.

For a time we made our way through a long, dark canyon. Why we hadn't risen directly from where the ship had been moored I didn't know, though I could guess. It was just that it was too close to home. No point in letting people know where you had your headquarters. When we were out of the mountains, Gallagher let the craft really rise, and we were up and away into the higher atmosphere.

It wasn't a fast journey such as the ones where you climb like an aircraft and begin breaking the sonic barrier almost before you've left ground. But there was an uncompromising thrill to the idea of a machine that could rise so buoyantly in the thin air and drift so silently yet powerfully in the direction it was commanded to go.

Eventually the ocean of atmosphere through which we had risen became almost as tenuous as the vacuum of space. At that point Gallagher cut in drives that were still quiet, but that produced a different motion in the ship. Again we began to climb.

I waited impatiently for hours to ask the questions I wanted to ask. I had thought to ask Suzie or Cricket, but they were stretched out sleeping on foam-rubber mats that lined the floor, as were the other men. Now Gallagher woke one of the men, turned over the controls to him, and stretched out. He was undoubtedly dead tired, but I had to know. I moved over beside him.

"How'd you capture it?" I asked softly.

"Didn't," he said. "It's ours." His voice was sleepy.

"But—"

"Told you I'd been tooling up for a revolution while we were on Betsy Ann. It was part of the tooling up."

"How'd it get here?"

"Came with us."

I was stumped. Gallagher had shrunk the
Glacier back nearly to its normal size before we
boarded her at Betsy Ann. I knew that. She
wasn't nearly as fat in the belly when we left
Betsy Ann as she had been made in order to
carry the refugees from Stellamira. And on the
way from Betsy Ann to Durango, I'd gone with
Gallagher all through the ship. There hadn't
been any holds of any real size, and even they
were practically empty. There hadn't been a
darned thing in the way of materials for a revolution, and that had both surprised and distressed
me, though I'd kept my mouth shut at the time.

Evidently the authorities on Durango had
been stumped, too. They'd sent up a boarding
party a few days after we'd escaped from the
port. They had been greeted only by Cricket.
They'd inspected the craft from end to end, and
then left, finding nothing but a bit of automatic
machinery on board, and a few small passages
and cabins.

They probably figured that Gallagher was
leaving the *Glacier* in synchronous orbit for use as
a radio relay through Cricket, and that by leaving it conspicuously alone they could tune in on
the communications.

It hadn't occurred to them, any more than it
had to me, that ice is a tricky substance—a
malleable material; that there might be more
holds and compartments that simply did not
connect either with the surface or with other
parts of the ship—bubbles in the ice that could

e opened into the rest of the ship or sealed off
rom it by the ice mice at any time.

One more question. "Have you built a solar-
ap base on the planet?"

"Wasn't time," he answered in a faraway
oice that signed him off as he fell asleep.

I worried the matter a long while, then fell
sleep myself so that when we reached the *Glacier*
ve were ready for action.

Gallagher didn't even pause in the control
oom when we reached the *Glacier*. He said,
"Bring us some food," to Suzie and then headed
ft. Seth stayed with Suzie, but Cricket followed
Gallagher and the seven men, and I tagged
long, handholding down the tunnels in free fall.

We entered a big open hold—open to space
nd to the planet below. And down the length of
he hold stretched a gigantic gun barrel, aimed
straight down. I shivered. Gallagher hadn't said
a word about that barrel—nor anything else, for
that matter—and I guess the thought that we
vere evidently going to pick off major cities—
well, it distressed me, but I kept my tongue.

The gun barrel and its associated equipment filled the hold. No, not filled. There was
space to work around it, but filled in the sense
that it was compacted with equipment.

Gallagher, Cricket, and the seven men went to
work. There was cryogenic equipment and aiming and focusing equipment, and most of it was
of a type with which I was familiar from my own
Space Academy days. But it was also sufficiently
unfamiliar that I knew without asking it would

be more trouble to clue me in than to use m
assistance. So I handed tools when asked, an
otherwise just watched.

Suzie and Seth brought food and we wen
through an airlock into a corridor to eat, but n
farther—just where we could take off ou
helmets. Then we went back, and Suzie and Setl
joined the work.

That gun was obviously one of the most pow
erful laser-beam generators I'd ever met. Th
power supplies and cryogenics equipment tha
filled that rather large cavity in the glacier wer
all more-or-less hidden by the shrouds and cov
ers that were necessary to keep stray radiatior
from straying and to keep the thing working a
top efficiency.

I learned later that it was a carbon dioxide-
type laser, but I didn't even know that mucl
about it while they were working on it.

No matter what any spaceman will tell you
about what feels like "up" and what feels like
"down" in free fall, if you're freefalling and
working—or even just standing beside—a long
thin barrel aimed at a planet, the planet has no
relationship of up or down to you. It's simply
"out there." That surprised me.

They seemed to be coming to the end of what
they were doing. Gallagher sent the seven men
inside, but Cricket kept working, and Suzie and
Seth just stepped back out of the way and
stayed. I kept quiet and stayed, too, hoping I
wouldn't be noticed.

Gallagher was sweating over some balance
controls that had been jury-rigged back to this

room from the main control cabin; and Cricket was taking impossibly fine readouts from the laser itself, using it in what I was sure was not its common mode of operation, as a low-powered ranging and detection unit.

"Swing angle is down now to about six centimeters at the far end of the beam. That makes it a lot less than a millisecond of arc, Gallagher. I think it's good enough."

"It makes it a lot less than I thought we could do," Gallagher replied, though he went on fiddling with the control board for a couple of minutes in rather grim silence. "Okay. What's the range now?"

"Swing is circular, around something like a six-centimeter diameter. Extreme range," Cricket read off a string of figures that ended in the word "centimeters," to which Gallagher replied, "Okay. Check and set. Upper range?"

There was another string of figures, which again ended in centimeters. "Okay. Check and set. Oscillator on. Check ranges."

The oscillator part I vaguely understood. A standard military laser has a zoom lens in the front end which brings it to a fine focus at a given distance. When you're firing at a target, the procedure is to bracket the estimated distance with that focal point, and then sweep back and forth through it. I hadn't been paying much attention to the near and far ranges as set, but it surprised me that they were being set in such close tolerance. Centimeters, yet, when in normal operation you would set them at plus or minus a hundred meters and simply sweep through whatever target you were aiming at.

Then I began recalling the figures and putting them together as approximations in my head. The sweep range between the two sets of figures was something like twenty-five kilometers—much as though an apprentice gunner were trying to hit a target whose distance he wasn't at all sure of. With a twenty-five-kilometer focal swing, the laser couldn't possibly concentrate enough energy for enough time in any one spot to be effective as a weapon. But in that case, why range it so carefully?

Gallagher glanced up at a large chronometer panel on the wall. "Still five minutes till time." His voice came through his helmet speaker.

"They won't mind if we start early," Suzie's voice came, and I glanced at her standing there with Seth protectively beside her. Not standing, really, since we were all in free fall. But the grace and poise that went with Suzie, and that even echoed massively in Seth, made it appear as though they were standing in a solid planetary field.

Gallagher chuckled quietly and told her that five minutes wasn't all that important and we could wait. So we did. Then . . .

"Okay, Cricket. Check the sweep."

The chronometer was just coming up on time as Cricket leaned forward and flipped a switch and the mechanical motion that drove the focusing lens structure in the front of the laser began putting out a middle C. *Cheeee. . .*

The sound sent shivers down my back, because it meant to me that an enemy had been sighted and was in range, though there seemed to be none of the tenseness here that you would find in the control room of a war vessel swinging up on target. And there was nothing but a planet out there for a target.

The ridiculousness of shooting a planet with the ineffective sting of a fine-focused laser began to creep up on me. The focus on this device was so fine that it would probably make no more than a centimeter-diameter hole in whatever target it hit, and though that's plenty big to play utter havoc with a space vehicle, it would be less than the sting of a mosquito so far as a planet was concerned.

"Set power pulse to three seconds."

Gallagher's voice was slightly edged, but Cricket's came back in a singsong that showed no overtones of emotion.

"Power pulse on three seconds by off point five seconds."

"Initiate pulse."

Cricket didn't have to respond to that one because the power machinery did it for her. There was a slow, rhythmic, *mmm-pop, mum-pop* from the power supply that went on and on and combined with the *cheeee* to form a now-familiar repetitive pattern; the song of power that I had heard on Betsy Ann: *cheee-ops, cheee-ops.*

"I'll be damned," I yelled. "This thing's an upside-down solar tap!"

There was a choke behind Gallagher's laugh, and his voice had a sweep and flow that spoke of tensions releasing.

"We're way above the radiation belts," he

said, "but the oscillating lens of our zoom focus makes an ionized path from Durango's ionosphere to its ground, and that's all you need for a tap. We didn't have time to build a pyramid down there, so we turned the tap upside-down."

And then I knew. Then I knew that we had won—that the battle was over and we had won.

There would not be a company electric plant on the whole planet of Durango that hadn't quit working in the last thirty seconds; for though broadcast power and hydroelectric power can work side by side, our side had obviously set its power to be antagonistic to the other.

I could picture in my mind's eye the frantic efforts of various power-plant officials all over the globe as they tried to find out why their fuses and circuit breakers were blowing like so much popcorn. They would not even know that broadcast power was a possibility—much less that it could have been established on Durango.

"Not even the spy-satellite system will be worth a damn now," I heard Cricket's satisfied voice over the intercom.

"And the port?" I asked, though I knew the answer.

"The port? Oh, much more than just the port." It was Suzie's voice this time, and it held a deep, inward joy. "The port's knocked out of course. But more. The effect reaches out several planetary radii. I'm quoting Gallagher," she added, "but he knows. It reaches out several planetary radii. Any ships that come close will be easy prizes—their electrical systems will be knocked out. Their motors and their instruments and . . . they can't even come close without our letting them."

I could see her face through her helmet, and she was beautiful. The lines were smoothed out, and there was only a quiet triumph and a peace such as I have seldom seen on a human being.

"We've won," she said. "We've won for Durango and for all the planets. We'll not be slaves again."

I stood there looking at them each—Cricket and Gallagher and Suzie and Seth, in their space suits in that ice chamber by that big barrel that pointed out through space to a planet. It took a minute for what Suzie had said to sink in.

Won for all the planets? But of course. When you can establish a power tap from outside, no corporation can keep the outside from coming in. They wouldn't have to set up pyramids on Durango or any of the other planets. They'd simply set up a satellite to take the place of the *Glacier,* and they'd surround it with smaller satellites to make a Jacob's ladder; and they could land their own ships. Land and take off. . . .

That deep, ringing voice that I heard—that *cheee-ops, cheee-ops, cheee-ops* of an upside-down tap —was a freedom bell ringing across the starways —modern, ruthless, *impertinent* to stupidity.

No, not impertinent. Just unforgiving of stupidity. And Earth and her colonial policies and her stop-motion bureaucracy and her dollar-sign cosmocorps were just plain stupid. Nature does not compromise with stupidity; and I guess modern man, or space man, or just plain technological man, can't compromise with it either. Not *won't*, just *can't*.

I looked at Suzie and I knew that she could quit the business of revolution now, and get on with the business of evolution. It was a business in which she'd be even more capable.

I looked at Cricket and I hoped that she'd want to get on with a different part of the business of evolution—the children part. I hoped that she'd know that children can be profitably raised on a spaceship, for I'm a spaceman and I'd make a poor groundling.

I looked at Seth, and I saw all his yearnings for a ship that was free in space coming true. It would probably be Gallagher's and Suzie's ship, but he'd be a free man in space, and that was what he wanted.

And I looked at Gallagher and I knew that it's men that make history, not history that makes a man. It takes a man to dream freedom so hard that the stupidities are brushed out of the way and mankind can follow. It takes a man to burst through the static forms that keep their shape by being rigid—the forms that can't change because any major change destroys them. It takes a man to replace that static stability with a dynamic stability that can change and adapt and grow and evolve.

It was then I began to feel the laughter that was bubbling up from my toes, and I knew finally what it is that makes a free man laugh. For there's the price of almost anything, and then there's the value. But the value at which I was looking is beyond price—the question of price simply drops out of the equation.

I looked down the barrel of that big freedom cannon pointing power for a planet and a pathway to the stars, and the laughter swooped up from my toes and enveloped me.

Comes a time when a man's got the right to lean back and laugh, tall and proud among the stars.

Welcome to the Future
Welcome to Destinies

THANK YOU, READERS ... for seeing that the first issue of DESTINIES went back to press even before it hit the stands —and the second looks like it may do the same! Readers are swept away by the world's very first paperback science fiction magazine—and by stories and articles by writers like these:

- POUL ANDERSON
- GREGORY BENFORD
- BEN BOVA
- ORSON SCOTT CARD
- JOE HALDEMAN
- DEAN ING
- LARRY NIVEN
- FREDERIK POHL
- JERRY POURNELLE
- SPIDER ROBINSON
- ROBERT SHECKLEY
- G. HARRY STINE

EDITED BY
James Baen

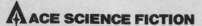

ACE SCIENCE FICTION   **$2.25**

POUL ANDERSON

48923	**The Long Way Home** $1.95
51904	**The Man Who Counts** $1.95
57451	**The Night Face** $1.95
65954	**The Peregrine** $1.95
69770	**Question and Answer** $1.50
91706	**World Without Stars** $1.50
91056	**The Worlds of Poul Anderson** $1.95
	THE SAGA OF DOMINIC FLANDRY
20724	**Ensign Flandry** $1.95
24071	**Flandry of Terra** $1.95

Available wherever paperbacks are sold or use this coupon.

Ace Science Fiction, Book Mailing Service,
Box 690, Rockville Centre, N.Y. 11571

Please send me titles checked above.

I enclose $ .... Add 50¢ handling fee per copy.

Name ....

Address ....

City .... State .... Zip ....

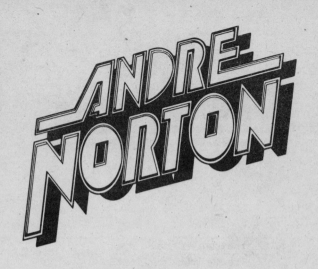

ANDRE NORTON

89705	**Witch World** $1.95
87875	**Web of the Witch World** $1.95
80805	**Three Against the Witch World** $1.95
87323	**Warlock of the Witch World** $1.95
77555	**Sorceress of the Witch World** $1.95
94254	**Year of the Unicorn** $1.95
82356	**Trey of Swords** $1.95
95490	**Zarsthor's Bane** (Illustrated) $1.95

Available wherever paperbacks are sold or use this coupon.

Ace Science Fiction, Book Mailing Service,
Box 690, Rockville Centre, N.Y. 11571

Please send me titles checked above.

I enclose $ . . . . Add 50¢ handling fee per copy.

Name . . . .

Address . . . .

City . . . . State . . . . Zip . . . .